D1073979

MEET THE
WITCHES

Georgess McHargue

MEET THE
WITCHES

J.B. Lippincott   New York

To Michael and Cerridwen

Photo credits: The Bettman Archive, 6; Essex Institute, Salem, Mass., 81, 96; Michael Holford, photographer/Victoria & Albert Museum, London, 43; Lennart Larsen, photographer/Danish National Museum, Copenhagen, 84; Librairie Larousse, Paris, 83; Jacqueline MacKay, 112; Mary Evans Picture Library, London, viii, 74; Picture Collection, The Branch Libraries, The New York Public Library, 13, 20, 24, 27, 32, 54, 60, 78; Staatliche Museen Zu, Berlin, 57; Samuel Weiser, Inc., York Beach, Me., 106.

Library of Congress Cataloging in Publication Data
McHargue, Georgess.
  Meet the witches.

  (Eerie series)
  Summary: Analyzes the phenomenon of witchcraft and discusses the various elements—primitive, classical, fairy-tale, pagan, historical, and modern—which have influenced its history.
  1. Witchcraft—Juvenile literature.   [1. Witchcraft]
I. Title.   II. Series.
BF1566.M37 1984   133.4′3   83-48446
ISBN 0-397-32071-X
ISBN 0-397-32072-8 (lib. bdg.)

          10 9 8 7 6 5 4 3 2 1
                  First Edition

Warning

This is a scary book. Witches in fairy tales eat children, and many peoples in the world today still believe that witches can make them sick or kill them. Furthermore, any book about witches has to talk about the time in our history when large numbers of real people were burned and tortured to death because they were accused of being witches.

If you don't mind all that because you're curious to know where we got our ideas about witches, you will enjoy this book. But if you have nightmares about being chased by people with pointy teeth and you get very nervous when a black cat crosses your path, you had better find something else to do. Above all, do not read this book at night when you are alone.

Contents

A typical Halloween witch. Illustrators borrowed her pointy hat from the sorcerer, who was supposed to have used it as a kind of megaphone down which imps and demons could squeak their messages.

1

The Weird Sisters

There are witches alive today.

That may seem a surprising way to begin a book on a scary subject such as witches. Most books about vampires, werewolves, ghosts, zombies, and so on quickly assure you that you will never meet a real one in the street. But witches are different.

One reason why they are different is that we may mean many things when we say the word "witch." Of course, the first thing most of us think of when witches are mentioned is that old dame with the pointy black hat, the cauldron, the broomstick, and the black cat. Often she has bats for friends and lives in a haunted house. She is famous for riding through the air on her broomstick and for casting spells, especially the kind that turn you into a toad or a turtle or a teapot. Every October, her picture appears on millions of paper napkins, cups, and plates, in advertisements and store windows, as rubber masks, and in books of cute stories that are generally about as frightening as "Goldilocks." This Halloween witch, as we may call her, gets many more giggles than shivers these days, and yet down deep we know that there is much more to witches than this.

Behind the Halloween witch, we can dimly see the shadowy forms of her sister witches, in a line that stretches back far, far beyond recorded history. We will be spending more time with each of them later, but let's introduce them briefly now.

By far the most ancient is the primitive witch, who may be hard for us to recognize as a witch at all. The primitive witch may be either a man or a woman, young or old, dressing and acting exactly like his or her friends and neighbors. Yet the primitive witch is believed to have the power and the will to harm others by magic. Today we may find primitive witches still at work in remote parts of Asia, Africa, the South Seas, or Central and South America, where people live without modern machines and technology, but the evidence is that belief in witchcraft has been found in every part of the world at one time or another.

Younger than the primitive witch, but still ancient, is the classical witch. She is so called after the classical period (roughly 500 B.C. to A.D. 400) of the Greeks and Romans, who believed in and wrote about her. Classical witches are almost always women, often beautiful women like the Greek Circe, who, in the ancient Greek epic poem *The Odyssey*, seduces the hero Odysseus and turns his men into swine.

Much more familiar to most of us is the fairy-tale witch, only a little younger than her classical sister. Yet, though everyone knows her, the fairy-tale witch is not much more like the Halloween witch than the classical and primitive witches are. For although they are old, ugly, female, and given to casting spells (spell-casting men in fairy tales are usually called sorcerers), fairy-tale witches don't dress like Halloween witches and would be quite likely to eat any children who were so foolish as to say to them, "Trick or treat!"

The fairy-tale witch has a sister so close as to be almost a twin, who is called the pagan witch. The pagan witch is actually a goddess who was thrown out of her sacred groves and temples when Christianity arrived in Europe, but who lived on in folktales, old customs, and superstitions.

Next is the historical witch, and here again we have someone who hardly seems related to the Halloween witch at all. Most of us know that at a certain period in European and American history, many very real individuals were accused of and arrested, tried, and executed for a supposedly very real crime called witchcraft. They were ordinary men, women, and even children of the 1500s and 1600s, and though we may call them historical witches, the evidence is that the vast majority of them were innocent victims of others' hatred and fear.

Finally, there is the modern witch (not to be confused with a Satanist), who may be a man or woman of any age, may live next door to you or me, and may be a housewife, doctor, policeman, student, union member, computer programmer, supermarket clerk, or any other normal-seeming member of society. Most modern witches are believers in a nature religion that emphasizes health, peace, and fertility and is strongly opposed to harmful and selfish uses of the magical and psychic powers sought by its members.

All of these witches, naturally, have influenced one another, and all of them except the modern witch, who has not been around long enough, have made large or small contributions to our picture of the Halloween witch. The names we have given the six types of witches are merely for our own convenience. The witches themselves and their neighbors neither knew nor cared about such distinctions.

As we go on to hear more about the various witches, we will find many fascinating clues to questions such as Why is the Halloween witch a woman? Where did she get her cat, cauldron, and hat? Why does she ride a broomstick? And why does she come out on October 31?

Before we go on to the next chapter, however, let's get the candy-corn taste of the Halloween witch out of our mouths and meet some proper witches (part pagan, part fairy-tale, and part historical) as they were described by the great English playwright William Shakespeare, whose plays give a wonderful picture of what people thought and how they viewed their world about four hundred years ago. One of Shakespeare's plays, *Macbeth*, is of special interest to us because it has three witches as characters.

The play is about a Scottish nobleman, Macbeth, who is led by ambition and greed to murder the king and seize the Scottish throne. That would not make much of a story if Macbeth were simply an evil man who did wrong. What makes the play interesting is that Macbeth has many doubts and fears about the terrible deed he plans, but is led on by his ruthless wife and by the prophecies of the three witches, who flatter him by foretelling that he will be "King hereafter." The witches are so important that they actually have the first scene of the play, which takes place on an open heath, or moor, during a thunderstorm. The witches speak briefly, planning a future meeting with Macbeth, when they will urge him on to the fateful murder of King Duncan.

An old lithograph shows Macbeth consulting the witches.

Then the First Witch exclaims, "I come, Graymalkin," the second says, "Paddock calls!" the third cries out, "Anon!" and they all disappear. It may be a puzzling little scene unless we know that in Shakespeare's time Graymalkin and Paddock were common names for a cat and a toad, respectively, just as today we may call a dog Rover, a cow Bossy, or a horse Dobbin. Thus nearly the first thing we learn about these witches is that their familiars are a cat and a toad, and that the animals can apparently call to them over long distances. Already, that sounds more like what we expect from a proper witch, and things get better as the play goes on.

In a later scene, the witches meet together again after an absence and offer one another neighborly greetings. "Where hast thou been, sister?" asks one. And the off-hand reply is "Killing swine." The First Witch, it develops, is working up her revenge on a woman who annoyed her by refusing to give her some chestnuts. Her plan is to sail in a sieve after the woman's sailor husband and keep him from returning home by raising a severe storm. Not exactly a group of sweet little old ladies! (But note that magical powers such as raising storms and sailing in sieves really belong to the pagan witch, although they sometimes turn up in fairy tales and in accusations against historical witches.)

The witches' biggest scene is in Act Four, which takes place in "... *a cavern. In the middle, a boiling cauldron.*" The three "weird sisters," as Shakespeare called them earlier, are in fact making witches' brew. This brew has some truly dreadful ingredients and is undoubtedly one of the most famous recipes in literature. (The numbers before the lines below will help us to refer back to them later.)

FIRST WITCH

1   *Round about the cauldron go.*

2   *In the poisoned entrails throw.*

3   *Toad, that under cold stone*

4   *Days and nights has thirty-one*

5   *Sweltered venom sleeping got,*

6   *Boil thou first i' th' charmed pot.*

ALL

7   *Double, double, toil and trouble;*

8   *Fire burn and cauldron bubble.*

SECOND WITCH

9   *Fillet of a fenny snake,*

10 *In the cauldron boil and bake;*

11 *Eye of newt and toe of frog,*

12 *Wool of bat and tongue of dog,*

13 *Adder's fork and blindworm's sting,*

14 *Lizard's leg and howlet's wing,*

15 *For a charm of pow'rful trouble,*

16 *Like a hell-broth boil and bubble.*

ALL

17 *Double, double, toil and trouble;*

18 *Fire burn and cauldron bubble.*

THIRD WITCH

19 *Scale of dragon, tooth of wolf,*

20	*Witch's mummy, maw and gulf*
21	*Of the ravined salt-sea shark,*
22	*Root of hemlock digged i' th' dark,*
23	*Liver of blaspheming Jew,*
24	*Gall of goat and slips of yew*
25	*Slivered in the moon's eclipse,*
26	*Nose of Turk and Tartar's lips,*
27	*Finger of birth-strangled babe*
28	*Ditch-delivered by a drab,*
29	*Make the gruel thick and slab.*
30	*Add thereto a tiger's chaudron*
31	*For th' ingredients of our cauldron.*

ALL

32	*Double, double, toil and trouble;*
33	*Fire burn and cauldron bubble.*

SECOND WITCH

36	*Cool it with a baboon's blood,*
37	*Then the charm is firm and good.*

Now *that* is a very witchy-sounding recipe, and it gets nastier when we understand it better. Some of the ingredients, to be sure, need no explanation. The animals mentioned, with few exceptions, are known for their fierceness or their nighttime habits and general creepiness. Nobody (in our society, at least, where we don't

9

eat reptiles) would be expected to accept a nice bit of lizard's leg or dragon scale with a polite thank-you. As for the other items, let's consider them line by line.

2   Entrails are guts. Yuck.

3–5   Toads do not have a poisonous bite, but many kinds produce an irritating substance in their skins that may be harmful to any animal that bites *them.* In Shakespeare's time, it was believed that a toad's poison was stronger after the animal had hibernated, or rested underground, where it would "swelter" or store up its venom. And why the thirty-one days? I can't really say, except that thirty-one rhymes better with stone than, say, thirty or twenty-eight. Even great poets sometimes have to stretch to get a good rhyme.

9   A fillet is a slice, and a fenny snake is one that lives in a fen, or marsh.

11   The newt is a harmless but crawly little creature that looks like a lizard but is more closely related to the frog.

12   Bats, of course, fly at night and so have always been associated with scary things and the dead. The dog may seem out of place here, but though we consider it a faithful friend, other times have seen it as a filthy and cowardly garbage eater.

13   The adder is a small poisonous snake that, like other snakes, has a forked tongue. The blindworm is

not a worm at all, but a legless lizard most often seen at night. It was incorrectly believed to have a sting.

14   A howlet is an owlet, or young owl, another creature of the night, ghosts, and graveyards.

20   Mummies are the preserved bodies of the dead, especially the ancient Eygptian dead. The existence of Egyptian mummies thousands of years old was well known in Shakespeare's time, and powdered mummy was a highly valued medicine, the idea being that what would preserve a dead body would also preserve a living one. Mummy powder was powerful, and a witch's mummy would seem to be even more so.

20–21   The maw and gulf are the mouth and throat; "ravined" means ravenous, that is, fierce and hungry.

22   The hemlock referred to is not the familiar evergreen tree, but a poisonous plant with a white flower. Like many poisons, it was thought to be more effective when gathered in the dark.

23 & 26   The people of Shakespeare's time held many religious and racial prejudices that we find wrong and foolish. Jews, Turks, Tartars, and others were feared because they had unfamiliar customs, and doubly feared because they were not Christians. The great conqueror Attila the Hun (a Tartar who died in A.D. 453) was known as "The Scourge of God" and was said in legend to be the son of a witch. That Shakespeare should in-

clude these items in his "hell-broth" is very interesting, since we shall see that a strong theme in the history of witchcraft is the desire to blame misfortunes on supposedly evil strangers, foreigners, or persons with special powers.

24   Gall comes from the gall bladder, an organ once thought to be the source of angry emotions. The goat is of course associated with the Devil because of its horns and hoofs.

24–25   Yew is a poisonous evergreen. Like the hemlock digged in the dark, it would be considered more powerful if cut during an eclipse of the moon, a bad-luck time when the dark night is even darker.

27–28   A baby born in a ditch of an unmarried mother was indeed a wretched little creature. One strangled at birth was even worse off, as it had not been baptized and its body could therefore be used for witchcraft. In mentioning the finger, Shakespeare may have been thinking of the Hand of Glory, a dreadful sort of candle made from the hand of a hanged man, by whose light evildoers were supposed to go about invisible.

29   Gruel is a sort of soup, and "slab" means thick.

30   "Chaudron" means guts again.

Now that the meaning of all the words is clear, go back and read the recipe a second time. Better still, read it aloud by the light of a single candle or outside a graveyard at dusk. The sound of the words alone is enough to make most people shiver, without quite knowing why. It's a good introduction to the world of primitive witchcraft, which is certainly a long way from that of the Halloween witch.

A picture of witches brewing a charm, from a book that appeared in Germany as early as 1508. It is easy to see where Shakespeare's Weird Sisters got some parts of their recipe.

2

The First Spear and the Second

Witchcraft is not a Western invention. Witchcraft is far older than our modern "Western" culture, far older than ancient Rome or Greece, far older even than the temples of China or the pyramids of Egypt. In fact, ancient history and studies of peoples who still live today without modern technology show that witchcraft beliefs have been almost as common on this earth as fear of the dark or dislike of snakes.

Witch beliefs have been found in every part of the world, and these beliefs are so similar that we can say something about what a "typical" witch belief is, whether it is found in tropical Africa, the islands of the South Seas, or the mountains of the South American Andes. If we were to ask a member of one of these "primitive" societies about witches, we would be told something like this: There are individuals in the world who exist only to harm others by magic. They are usually born with this power, and in many cases they cannot help doing evil, just as the rattlesnake cannot help biting you if you step on it. Primitive witches, as we may call them, are usually adults, although some are children, and they are about as likely to be men as to be women. Nevertheless, there are many individual societies where witches are of one or the other sex only. Sometimes one may tell who is a witch by a bodily sign such as the fact that the individual has red eyes. Sometimes, the doctors or medicine men declare that if one cuts open a dead witch one will find a snake or other harmful creature in the belly, or perhaps a special witch organ that is not found in other people. As individuals, witches are often cold, quarrelsome, or stingy.

Witches have been accused of causing almost every kind of misfortune, but some accusations are much more common than others. In addition to the sicknesses and deaths of individuals, primitive witches are especially likely to bring on disasters that affect the whole community, such as droughts, storms, floods, and plagues of insects. In the Trobriand Islands of the South Pacific, the people once went so far as to insist that *every* death was caused by witchcraft, including suicides and obvious accidents.

The most likely victims of witches are their own families and neighbors; witches rarely attack strangers. They act out of spite, jealousy, or a desire for revenge. In some cases, they seem to have no reason for their evil acts but general desire to do harm. More often than not, they don't even stand to profit by their witchcraft. For them, to misquote an old saying, "Evil is its own reward."

Witches always work in secret, usually at night, when they may leave their bodies peacefully asleep in their huts while their spirits flit about doing harm. When they cause sickness and death in this manner, they are often described as eating their victims' souls. This type of witch is not really very different from a vampire. Night-flying witches may also be invisible or appear as mysterious lights or were-creatures, of which the werewolf is only the best known. The most popular form for a witch to take is that of the owl, bat, vulture, or other creature associated with darkness or the dead.

Besides practicing witchcraft, these primitive witches have other habits that can make us shudder. They frequently eat human flesh and prefer that of their own families. They may also eat corpses, go naked, commit incest, and refuse to be toilet trained.

There is nothing comical about these primitive witches, and nothing to sneer at, either. We human beings are amazing creatures, who can be deeply affected by what goes on in our minds. If you *know* (I don't say suspect, or even fear, but know for certain) that witchcraft can kill you, then there is a chance you may in fact die if you think you are bewitched. There have been actual individuals who died in spite of everything Western doctors could do to save them, because their nervous systems could not stand the strain of their own terror. It is important to remember throughout this book that *to those who believe in it, witchcraft can kill.*

Perhaps now beneath the pointy hat and black cape of the Halloween witch, we can see something much older and more terrifying. To any group of people that believes in witchcraft, the witch, male or female, is nothing less than each society's private nightmare, the kind of person it hates and fears, a traitor within the family or village. The witch does *only* what is not permitted. In societies where generosity is valued, the witch is tight-fisted; where children are taught to practice self-control, the witch is noisy and boisterous; where food is always hoarded against a bad season, the witch may be one who is foolishly generous. I do not know of any witchcraft studies that have been done in cannibal societies (few if any are left today), but one may suppose that in such a case the witch would be someone who *refused* to eat "long pig."

At other times and in other places, however, witchcraft accusations have related to economic and social concerns rather than to moral ones. In the Mysore (now Karnataka) province of India, for instance, a great increase in witchcraft accusations came about a few decades ago, after an irrigation system made it possible for some of the local women to become moneylenders because they no longer had to work in their husbands' fields. They used the time to increase their dairy cattle herds, sold the milk for money, and lent their earnings at interest to the poorer farmers of the community. Suddenly the women had power over the men, and the men did not like it. When some of the men found that they could not pay back the loans, a rash of witchcraft accusations broke out, many of them against those same women who had become moneylenders. No one suggested that the men simply didn't want to pay their debts, and the men themselves were sure they were completely in the right. All their lives, they had been taught that men were superior to women. Now if the women had more power than they did, it could only be because some evil force was at work. The women *had* to be witches and deserved to be punished, and that was the only way the people of Mysore province were prepared to look at things. They would no doubt have laughed if anyone had tried to tell them that their troubles sprang not from witchcraft but from economics, which is to say that in this particular case, the witch scare was set off by a change in the way money was made and lost.

Witchcraft outbreaks quite often have economic reasons behind them (although social and religious concerns can also be important), and usually they mean trouble for those individuals who are believed, rightly or wrongly, to have gained an unfair advantage over their neighbors. Yet strangely enough, there are some cases in which fear of witchcraft may have done more good than harm to the community at large. Among the Navajo Indians, for example, the belief that the old may bewitch one has certainly encouraged some individuals to be more generous to the elderly than they might otherwise have been.

Similarly, but more gruesomely, the Nyakusa of West Africa believe that witches are principally moved by a fierce hunger for meat and milk (foods not always easy to come by in that part of Africa). Nyakusa witches may turn themselves into pythons and gnaw their victims to death from inside, or they may fly about at night stealing milk from cattle, which then "dry up" and fail to bear calves. The Nyakusa say that witches choose as their victims people who have offended them. Thus they teach their children that the good person is one who gets on well with everyone and who is generous with the meat and milk from the family herd. It pays, therefore, not to be stingy or quarrelsome in Nyakusa society, for, as a local saying declares, "Well-fed pythons stay quiet," which is as much as to say that the generous are not threatened by witchcraft.

Yet, although the fear of witchcraft occasionally seems

Taken in South Africa in 1897, this photograph allegedly shows a witch doctor, although that cannot now be verified. Note that one of the skulls is not human. Gorilla?

to serve useful purposes in certain cases, we must come back to the fact that the first and most important thing witchcraft beliefs do is to explain what we today would probably call accident or chance misfortune. The Azande people of central Africa look at the matter like this: The hunter who spears the game always shares the meat with the hunter who cast the second spear. They are considered to have killed the animal together. Thus if a man is killed by a charging elephant, the Azande say that the elephant is only *the first spear*. Witchcraft is always the second spear, the hidden cause of the accident. This outlook has the advantage of explaining events that would otherwise remain mysterious. "Why was it *my* child who drowned, *my* house that burned down?" No matter how tragic an event may be, it is easier to blame someone else for it than to think that it "just happened."

The problem, of course, arises with the need to find and punish the witch. There really are a great many things in the world—even tragic things—that happen purely by chance, which means that the "witch" who is blamed for them is innocent and is being unfairly punished or, sometimes, killed. Furthermore, the idea that misfortunes are caused by witchcraft can lead people into all sorts of false reasoning, as a wise old man of the African Gusii tribe once explained:

Suppose there is a cattle plague. Nearly all of my cattle die, but my neighbor loses only a couple of beasts. I wonder whether he has bewitched me; it was strange that I should lose so many, and he only so few. Now my neighbor has seen that I am still able to lead out my plough with a pair of strong oxen, but the plague killed just those two animals of his that he always used for ploughing. He says to himself how strange it is that I can still plough and not he. Perhaps I am the one who has bewitched him.

Thus, to believers in witchcraft, anyone may be a witch, and the same event may lead two parties to accuse *each other,* whereas neither is in fact to blame. This is the price in injustice, suffering, and suspicion, that must be paid by any society in return for accepting witchcraft beliefs. In some cases, it is true, witchcraft may be believed in and frequently spoken of without any actual accusations being made or vengeance taken, but as we saw above in the example from India, a change in the life of the community may bring about an outbreak of accusations (often with accompanying violence) like that which took place in Europe during the witch trials.

This is not to say, of course, that persons accused of witchcraft are always innocent. There is no doubt at all that certain individuals have actually practiced witchcraft, and done so quite recently in places such as Africa, South America, and the islands of the Pacific Ocean, and newspapers still carry occasional stories headed "Witch Murder," although the victim in such cases is nearly always the accused witch, not a witch's victim.

(There are people who describe themselves as witches at work in our Western society also, as we will see in Chapter Eight.)

Sometimes, an accused witch is found to be in possession of sinister items that have no known use except in witchcraft. Much more rarely, a witch may even confess his or her witchcraft to an outsider and demonstrate the "tricks of the trade." Certainly anyone who would willfully practice magic for the purpose of harming someone else is a person you wouldn't want to have around, especially since poison is one form of "magic" that can actually work. Nevertheless, the real witches must be many fewer than those accused of witchcraft. One scientist was able to examine a large collection of supposedly magical objects that had been gathered from a village of the Bemba people in what was then called Rhodesia (now Zimbabwe), Africa. The objects had been collected by *Bamucapi*, members of a special group of "witch finders" who periodically go through the area in much the way that a gardener may go over the lawn or garden spreading weed killer. The comparison is quite a good one, because just as weed killer is supposed to kill weeds and leave the grass alone, so the magical *mucapi* medicine of the Bamucapi is supposed to be harmless to nonwitches but to cause any witch to die a horrible death. When the Bamucapi come around, they

So-called "gregree men" of West Africa, famed for the manufacture of amulets to keep away witches.

search out or are given all the supposed witch charms in the village and they pile them up outside the village to show what terrible danger the village was in before they came.

(This is a good place to clear up a common misunderstanding about African life. "Witch doctors" serve a function rather like that of the Bamucapi. They cure victims of witchcraft; they do not practice witchcraft themselves. To confuse witch doctors with witches, as non-Africans often do, is like confusing policemen with burglars.)

Of the one hundred thirty-nine objects collected by the Bamucapi and examined by anthropologist Audrey Richards, as mentioned above, only fourteen turned out to be of the sort that might actually have been used by witches. All the others were containers of harmless medicines or good luck charms of the kind worn and used by nearly everyone. Thus it seems that only about one out of every ten accusations made by the Bamucapi (or 14 out of 139) may have been true. Probably the number of true accusations would be even smaller in a hysterical atmosphere like that of the much later European witch trials, as opposed to the almost routine operations of the Bamucapi (and of the many similar witch-finding societies that exist in Africa and elsewhere). In most cases, whether modern or ancient, African or European, it seems to be in the nature of things that the innocent should far outnumber the guilty among those accused of witchcraft.

3

The Worst
Witch Story of All

Belief in witchcraft was probably held in common by many of our earliest ancestors the world over, and the most interesting thing about witch beliefs is how little they really changed over hundreds, and even thousands of years. By the time of the ancient Greeks and Romans (roughly 500 B.C. to A.D. 400), people in the Western world no longer lived a simple life of farming and hunting, but had created cities, governments, money, politics, and international trade not too much different from those today, though on a smaller scale. Yet ideas about witches had not changed greatly from those described in the last chapter.

The story we are about to read was written down by a Roman named Lucius Apuleius (ap-yuh-LEE-us), who was born around A.D. 125. Apuleius evidently knew a good deal about magic, for one of the few facts we have about his life is that his in-laws took him to court on the charge that he had bewitched his wife. As you read

An illustration of the Greek style for a modern edition of Homer's Odyssey. *The charming witch Circe offers wine to Odysseus. Only her possibly magical staff may reveal her as more than a good hostess.*

the story, think about the habits of primitive witches, and you will see that, if you leave out the fine buildings of the classical period, there is nothing in the story that would be out of place in a tale of primitive witchcraft.

The narrator of the story is a young man named Thelyphron (TEL-i-fron).

"While I was still a student at the university," recounts Thelyphron, "I felt a desire to visit northern Greece. I traveled through most of Thessaly, and by the time I reached Larissa I had very little money left. That was an unlucky day for me. As I was wandering about, I saw a tall old man making a public announcement in the marketplace. He was offering a large reward to anyone who would stand guard over a certain corpse that night. 'What's all this about?' I asked a fellow standing near me. 'Do the dead bodies of Larissa generally jump up and walk away?'

" 'Not so loudly, boy. I can see you are a stranger here, or you wouldn't have to ask about our Thessalian witches, who are so bold that they often attack corpses and gnaw bits of flesh off their faces for use in their magic spells.'

" 'Oh, really? And what does one have to do to guard a Thessalian corpse?'

" 'First of all, you have to watch it carefully, every minute of the night, without looking away even once. You see, the witches can change their shapes whenever they want to. They can be dogs or birds or mice or even flies, and they do it so well that no one could tell the difference from the real thing—no, not even in broad daylight, in a court of law. And if you look at one of them, she will bewitch you. I don't dare go into all the horrid tricks they can use in order to get at a corpse. Anyway, in my opinion, the usual reward of 100 to 150 drachmas [Greek money] is hardly worth the horrible risk. Oh, and I forgot to say that if the corpse isn't found whole in the morning, the guard will have pieces of his own face cut off to supply the missing bits. That's according to our law.'

"This tale was not of a kind to frighten me, however, and I went straight up to the old man and told him I was the fellow he was looking for. 'What is the fee?' I asked him.

" 'A thousand drachmas,' he replied, 'and it's none too much, believe me, for the dead man was the son of one of our most prominent citizens. Those foul hags the witches always take special pleasure in attacking those who are famous, rich, or handsome, and he was all three.' The old man gave me no time to change my mind then, but hurried me off to a big house, in through a small side door, and along some corridors until we came to the death chamber, a room with drawn shutters where a woman in black sat wailing the dead. When the old man had told her who I was, she pushed the hair back from her face (she was very beautiful, as I could not help noticing) and begged me to guard her husband well. Then she showed me the corpse, lying on a slab and wrapped in a white linen shroud, and to my surprise she called in seven of the mourners as well as her secretary and made them all bear witness in writing that the corpse was whole when it was entrusted to me. Then, sooner than I really liked, I found myself alone with the corpse and a burning lamp.

"Night came on and shadows gathered in the corners of the room, but I stayed awake by rubbing my eyes and kept my spirits up by singing loudly. All the sounds of the household had died away and the time was nearing midnight. I had been no more than a little nervous at first, but now I was getting to like the cold and the silence and the flickering of the lamp less and less.

"Suddenly I saw the thin, sleek body of a weasel slink in through a hole in the door. Before I could move, the beast had run right into the room and stopped a few feet from me, staring at me with her shiny black eyes. This unnatural behavior had me thoroughly alarmed, but I roused myself and shouted at her, whereupon she ran out of the room. However, as soon as she had gone, I felt sleep pull me down into its depths as if I had been a sinking stone. I lay a long time on the floor, as still as the body on the slab—two corpses, in fact, without a guard.

"At last the light of dawn began to show, and I awoke in terror, grabbed the lamp, and carried it to the slab. To my huge relief, however, the corpse's face, when I pulled back the shroud, was quite whole. Just then the widow returned with the seven witnesses and the secretary, and she wept most bitterly over the corpse and kissed it when she saw it was unharmed. 'I thank you for your loyal services, young man,' she said while the secretary counted out my fee, and I, delighted with my good fortune, replied, 'Madam, I shall be very pleased to help you again, whenever you may need my assistance.'

"At this, the whole household turned on me with shouts and curses, and I realized what a tactless thing I had said. Still, as I collected myself in the street outside, I remembered that I still had my fee, and that was what mattered. Out of curiosity, I decided to wait around to see the corpse carried to its last resting place, for a man of such importance was likely to be honored by a public procession. Indeed, a considerable crowd turned up, and I followed along toward the marketplace, where I was in time to see an old gentleman come running up with tears streaming down his face and his hair and clothing torn in sign of mourning. Like a madman he rushed up to the coffin and cried to the crowd, 'I appeal to you for vengeance! I appeal to you for justice! This poor nephew of mine has been killed—murdered—by that evil woman who stands before you as his widow. She poisoned him because she had taken a lover and wanted her husband's estate. She and she alone is the murderess!'

Classical witches sometimes had horses' hoofs, as in the scene above. Note that the witch on the right holds a limbless "doll," perhaps of the sort used for working spells on victims from a distance.

"What a scene took place then: the old man accusing, the widow weeping and denying her guilt, and the crowd shouting and taking sides, some wanting to burn the witch, some to silence the uncle. At last it was agreed to submit the case to the judgment of the gods, and the uncle, with an air of triumph, led forth an impressive man, robed in white and with shaven head, whom he introduced as Zatchlas the Egyptian. 'He is one of the leading magicians of his country,' the uncle declared, 'and he promises, for a large fee, to recall my nephew's soul from the underworld so that we may learn the truth. I do not seek to reverse fate, nor to deny to the grave what is its due. I beg for my nephew only a brief return to the living so that he can help me avenge his murder—the only comfort I can find in my overwhelming grief.'

"At this the crowd stood back and fell silent while the magician made his preparations for the solemn and terrible deed that was to be done. He touched the mouth of the corpse three times with a magical herb, and placed another on its breast. Then, turning to the east, he prayed silently to the rising sun. The crowd gasped and an expectant hush fell over the marketplace. I myself pushed through the crowd and climbed up on a stone that stood just behind the coffin, in order to get a better view.

"In a few moments the corpse was seen to breathe and color returned to the face. The young man then sat up, and the magician questioned him about the manner of his death. With a groan, he replied, 'Why could you not let me alone when I had at last cast off the troubles of this world? Must I come back to witness my shame? My wife has already replaced me with another. The one whom I held most dear bewitched and poisoned me.'

"This speech only raised more argument among the bystanders. Some were for burying the wife in her husband's grave. Others held that the evidence of a senseless corpse was not to be trusted.

"The corpse, seeming to tire of the matter, gave another loud groan and declared, 'Very well, I will settle the matter once and for all. I will tell you something that is known to no man living.'

"Then suddenly he pointed at me. 'While that student was guarding my corpse, the ghoulish witches slipped into the room, even though the doors were locked. They came in the form of weasels and mice, and they threw a sleeping spell over him so that he fell to the floor as one dead. Then they called me by name, and I should by their wicked arts have been forced to obey, only that it chanced that the poor student has the same name as myself, Thelyphron. Thus when the witches called me, and while my stiffened limbs were trying to obey them, he rose up and gave himself to their horrible purpose. And as witches will, they gnawed off first his nose and then his ears. But to hide what they had done, they left him with a nose and ears made of wax, and to this moment the poor fellow thinks he has been generously rewarded for a job well done, not knowing he has been cast out upon the world to frighten it with his ghastly face.'

"Then, and only then, did I clap my hands to my face.

"My nose fell off, and then my ears. . . ."

4

Fairy Tales, Fox-Witches, and Zombies

The first thing we have to understand about fairy tales and the witches in them is that such tales were not made up by any one person and were not written down for hundreds (in some cases, many hundreds) of years after they were first told. Scholars now believe that fairy tales contain some very ancient ideas, memories, and bits of lore that can give us important clues to customs, events, and beliefs that are otherwise unknown to us, although such evidence has become so confused over the centuries that it must be treated with caution. Still, it would be a mistake to think that fairy tales are just amusing stories for the young. Many are exciting, frightening, or inspiring, rather than amusing, and few if any were intended for children.

The fairy tale of Hansel and Gretel and their adventures with the wicked witch in her candy-and-gingerbread house is so well known that it will be a good place to start if we want to find out what Western fairy-tale witches are like. The version of "Hansel and Gretel" written down more than a hundred years ago by the brothers Grimm in Germany tells quite a lot about fairy-tale witches in general.

First of all, Hansel and Gretel's witch lived in the middle of a deep, dark forest, and while fairy-tale witches do not always live in forests, they do tend to be found in lonely and frightening places. In the Grimms' version, the witch is described only as an old woman leaning on a crutch, and at first she speaks nicely to the children in order to lure them into her house. In fact, the story says that the witch made a habit of trapping children this way, using candy as bait. She always knew when children were near, for although her eyes were red and she was nearsighted, she had a keen sense of smell like an animal's. Thus she may remind us of the giant at the top of Jack's beanstalk, with his cry of "Fe, fi, fo, fum,/ I smell the blood of an Englishman."

Like the giant, this witch ate people, and even went to some trouble to fatten Hansel up for her table. She intended to eat Gretel also, but first made her do the housework, such as fetching water and cooking. Finally, clever Gretel got the witch to climb into her own oven, where she was burned up. It's interesting to find a fairy-tale witch being burned, since convicted historical witches were frequently burned at the stake. In both cases the underlying idea is that a dead witch (or vampire, or werewolf) may come back to life from even the tiniest fragment of bone or flesh. Thus the idea was not only to kill the witch, but to scatter the ashes to the four winds.

After destroying the witch, Hansel and Gretel returned joyfully home, but not without taking something with them. For in every corner of the house stood "chests of pearls and precious stones." Here is another characteristic of fairy-tale witches: they often possess treasures.

If we are curious to know just where witches get their wealth, we may find a hint in the German tale "Lazy Hans." There the witch owns a magic staff that, if placed upright in a cornfield, will cause all the corn to fly into the witch's barn or, if planted in a dairy, will cause all the milk churns to do as the corn did. With magic like that, witches clearly have no need to work for a living. This story can't help but remind us of the way witchcraft works in primitive societies, and especially the way it is sometimes connected to envy of one's more prosperous neighbors.

The one thing about Hansel and Gretel's witch that makes her different from most fairy-tale witches is that she does not actually *bewitch* anybody; that is, she does not transform people into animals or give them human shapes other than their own. In many of our most familiar fairy tales, it seems that witches spend much of their time bewitching people, often by means of a spell or magical saying. The unfortunate young man in "The Frog Prince" is of course condemned to be green spotted, web-footed, and bulgy eyed by a witch's spell; and it was also a witch who made the little magic shirts that turned the six brothers into "The Six Swans." The same Lazy Hans mentioned above is turned into a pig and a goose, while unwanted stepchildren are bewitched into a "Lambkin and Little Fish" in the tale of that name, and in "The Crystal Ball" the witch turns two of her own sons into an eagle and a whale. In short, there is no apparent end to the fairy-tale witch's powers of transformation. When convenient, she can also transform herself, like the witch in "Jorinda and Joringel," who goes about in the form of a cat or a screech owl at night. This is interesting, because the historical witches were often accused of having "familiars"—ordinary animals such as cats, dogs, mice, or insects, who had the very extraordinary power of talking with the witch or doing her bidding. Sometimes the witch was even supposed to transform herself *into* the familiar, the better to work her evil will. We have already seen that primitive witches are often supposed to take the forms of animals, especially night-flying ones such as the bat and the owl.

As we will see in the next chapter, however, the power to transform *other people* into animals properly belongs to goddesses rather than to witches.

We can see, then, that the Halloween witch got her spells and her age and her possible fondness for eating children from the fairy-tale witch, but we are still a long way from the pointy hats, cauldrons, cats, and broomsticks we have come to expect from a "real" witch.

Before we go on to learn more about the other weird sisters—the pagan witch and the historical witch—let's remind ourselves what a properly scary fairy-tale witch was all about. This story comes straight from the brothers Grimm, but you won't find it in very many modern fairy-tale books because most adults think it is too frightening for children. It is obviously a story that was told by parents to make their kids behave, just the way Little Orphant Annie warned, in James Whitcomb Riley's poem, "The gobble-uns'll git you/Ef you don't watch out." As you read this story, remember that the people who ran the witch trials that executed thousands of people in Europe a few hundred years ago had been brought up on stories very much like this one.

THE OLD WITCH

Once there was a stubborn, willful little girl who always

wanted her own way and would never listen to her parents. How could she be happy? One day she said to her parents, "You keep telling me about this old witch; I think I'll go and visit her. I've heard she's really a wonderful old woman with fascinating things in her house, and I want to see them."

The parents, of course, forbade her to go. "The witch is an evil old woman who does dreadful things. If you have anything to do with her, we will never speak to you again," they said.

But the little girl wouldn't listen, and went skipping straight off to the witch's house. When she got there, the old woman let her in and asked her why she looked so pale. "Oh, granny," said the little girl, "I'm pale with fright because of what I've just seen."

"And what was that?" asked the witch.

"I saw an all-black man on your steps."

"That was just the man who delivers the coal," said the witch.

"And then I saw a man who was all gray."

"That was just a sportsman in his hunting clothes," said the witch.

"And then I saw a blood-red man."

"That was just the butcher bringing the meat," said the witch.

"Oh, but the worst thing was when I peeked through

the window and there, sitting before the fireplace, was not you but a terrible creature with a fiery head."

"Then you have seen the witch as she really is," said the witch. "I have waited for you a long time and now someone will get some use out of you." And she snatched the child and changed her into a block of wood. Then the old witch threw the wood on the fire and sat down comfortably to warm herself. "Now for once that dratted fire is burning well," she muttered.

It's interesting to wonder whether Shakespeare had heard this story or one like it, for at the end of one of the scenes in *Macbeth* he has his witches sing a song that goes, "Black spirits and white, red spirits and gray,/ Mingle, mingle, mingle, you that mingle may"—exactly as if he had in mind the black, red, and gray men on the Old Witch's doorstep.

Of course, not all witch tales are Western. Just as primitive witchcraft beliefs can be found on every continent, so folktales about witches can be found around the world. Japanese and Chinese witches, for example, are most often said to be foxes—that is, they can appear as either human beings or foxes, and in human form, whole families of them may live side by side with ordinary people. They could thus be called werefoxes, just as persons who can transform themselves into wolves

Japanese print by Kuniyoshi. A man is confronted by an apparition of the fox-goddess, who appears in folklore as a witch.

are werewolves. "Were-" means man or manlike.

Most famous of the Japanese fox-witches was Tamamo-no-Maye, who could appear either as a beautiful court lady or as an ancient fox with an eight-forked tail. Her favorite pastime was to fascinate the ruler of a powerful state and ruin the country by tempting him to sin. It was said she had already brought disaster to India and China when she arrived in Japan by flying across from the Chinese mainland. However, before she could gain power over the emperor, her evil ways were discovered by a wise nobleman who overcame her with the help of a magical mirror. In the mirror, the witch no longer appeared beautiful, but returned to her true form, whereupon an army of warriors sprang out of the mirror and chased her until she took refuge in a rock that stood on the plains of Nasu. For many years thereafter, the rock was known as the Death Stone, and every living thing that touched it was killed instantly, or so the legend says.

Thus the Japanese fox-witch has another characteristic that links her to the vampire, namely, that she has no power over a mirror. The reason is that one may bedazzle the mind of a mere human being, but a mirror can reflect only the truth. In fact, there is good reason to say that vampires and werewolves are really only particular kinds of witches, since witches are much more ancient than the other two types of beings.

Oddly enough, considering how widely witches are, or were until recently, believed in in Africa, there are not a great many African tales dealing with witchcraft. Those that do exist are unusual because they describe witches as acting in groups and even having gatherings such as historical European witches were accused of holding, but which do not occur in European tales. African witches, in some places, are supposed to gather together in order to dig up the dead, whom they bring back to life and cause to carry out their orders. Eventually, these unfortunate dead are eaten by the witches, and in fact there is some confusion in the tales as to whether the main purpose of reviving corpses is to eat them.

Anyone who has watched late-night TV horror movies will know right away that the beings described above are often called zombies. Indeed, belief in zombies plays quite an important role in the folklore of the Caribbean islands and Central and South America, where it was brought by African slaves. For our purposes, it is important to note that zombies (they have many other names in Africa) are not witches themselves, but only their helpless victims. Nevertheless, they have interesting powers, which are derived from those of witches. Thus, among the African Zulu, the "undead" are called *umkovu*. In order to make an umkovu, the witches (both men and women) give the corpse certain magic medicines, pierce the forehead with a hot needle, and slit the tongue so that the creature can only mumble. Umkovu can be heard at night outside the villages, shrieking and howling, terrifying everyone within earshot. They have the power to make the grass entangle the feet of night-time travelers, thus holding them up until the umkovu can catch them, kill them, and enroll them in their horrid ranks. It is no wonder that, since they had to deal with actual lions, hyenas, and leopards, as well as with witches and their undead servants, very few people used to go out at night in that part of Africa.

5

Meet the Pagan Witch

It is obvious that the fairy-tale witches of the last chapter are quite different from either primitive witches or classical witches. We can still see in them the outlines of the primitive witches with their general ill will toward humankind and their tendency to eat souls or the bodies of the dead, but where did they get their powers of bewitchment, their preference for children as victims, and their strong tendency (strongest in Europe but present also in China and Japan) to be women rather than men?

What had happened between the period of primitive witchcraft beliefs, which were probably held by our earliest ancestors the world over, and the fairy-tale witches was simply a few thousand years of human religious history. People's ideas about who made the universe and how it works have changed greatly and often over the centuries. But such changes are almost never neat and complete. One tribe conquers another tribe and announces, "Okay, you folks are going to worship our gods now." Sometimes the new gods may just quietly take over the temples and ceremonies of the old ones, often because both peoples recognize, "Hey, our moon goddess is really just like your moon goddess." At other times, things are not so simple. Then, when the principal god of the conquerors is male, he may be said to have married the goddess of the conquered. A third possibility is that the conquerors may have a really hard time getting the conquered to adopt their gods, and then their priests or priestesses may preach the idea that the old gods were not gods at all, but evil demons. Sometimes, all three of these processes go on at once, and after hundreds or thousands of years, the mythology and folktales of the region can become very confusing indeed.

In the Japanese tale of the fox-witch told in the last chapter, we may suspect that fox-people may not originally have been witches, for the very end of the story is that a holy monk (a Buddhist) cast the evil creature out of the stone so that it ceased to be dangerous, a very typical ending for a tale from a culture where one religion has replaced another. Stories of early Christian saints are full of similar victorious duels with trolls, giants, sea monsters, dragons, mermaids, and other beings who, like the witch, have the misfortune to belong to an earlier period of religious history.

It seems clear that witches in the fairy tales of both East and West have been subject to processes like those described above, particularly the last one. That is, witches have been given characteristics that originally belonged to goddesses in the days before Christianity came to Europe and Buddhism or Islam to the Orient.

If we want to look for pre-Christian roots for Western witches, we can consider the goddesses of the pagan Celts (ancestors of most modern Irish, Welsh, Scots, Cornish, and Bretons). Celtic goddesses were remarkable and powerful beings, quite unlike the graceful deities of later Greek and Roman mythology, with whom we are more familiar. The Irish Badhbh was a goddess of battle, who often took the form of a raven, a bird that gathers around battlefields to feed on corpses. Like most goddesses, including the Greek ones, Badhbh had many other names. As Medhbh, she led an army against Ulster, and her very appearance was so horrifying that warriors who saw her lost two thirds of their courage. As the Morrigan she was discovered by the Daghdha, the Irish father god, washing the clothing of those who are about to die in the battle of Mag Tuiredh. In this incident, she demonstrates a power commonly found among Celtic warrior goddesses and later attributed to witches—that of foretelling the future. She also reminds us of the banshee, the supernatural "washer at the ford" of Scottish and Irish folklore.

The Celtic goddesses have another interesting characteristic: they tend to come in threes. In some tales, in fact, Badhbh has two sisters with the same name. There are also many carvings showing goddesses with three faces, or in groups of three. This love of threes can be found in ancient religions from Ireland to India, but is especially strong in Celtic countries. Goddesses were often thought of as having three forms—maiden, mother, and hag. As such, they represent the three stages of any woman's life, so it is not strange that they are seen as acting independently even though they are one and the same. But clearly it is the hag member of the trio who has become the witch. In this connection, we should also remember the Norns, the three Norse fate goddesses who spun, wove, and snipped the threads of life. Their names, Urd, Verdandi, and Skuld, mean past, present, and future, and they are very similar to the three Parcae of the Romans. Perhaps we can now understand why Shakespeare's weird sisters are three, rather than four or two or five.

Another, different sort of Celtic goddess is the Welsh Cerridwen. In the principal story about her, she brewed a great cauldron full of the broth of wisdom and immortality, intending it for her son. She set a boy named

Gwion to stir the broth, and he accidentally tasted three drops of it, thus gaining all its benefits. The first thing his newfound wisdom told Gwion was that he should run from the anger of Cerridwen. He changed himself into a swift hare, but she chased after him as a greyhound; he became a fish and she an otter; he a bird and she a hawk. Finally, he became a grain of wheat and Cerridwen, as a sharp-eyed hen, swallowed him. Later, in the form of a white sow ("Cerridwen" means white sow in Welsh), she went about the country giving the people gifts of grain, bees, and her own piglets.

There are many things in this story of Cerridwen that remind us of witchcraft. Here is a woman with a cauldron—one full, not of poison, but of wisdom and everlasting life. (The idea of a life-giving cauldron is quite common in Indo-European mythologies.) Possibly the brew in the cauldron turned to poison after the worship of Cerridwen was forbidden by the Church.

But though the original Cerridwen was wise, she could also be frightening. She could turn herself into various animals (as historical witches were accused of doing) and even swallowed the child Gwion like a fairy-tale witch. Finally, she controlled many aspects of farm life, giving magical gifts of useful animals and grain. (Her connection with pigs makes us think of the classical witch Circe, who turned the sailors of the hero Odysseus into swine.) Indeed, the story is intended to show that Cerridwen *invented* agriculture, beekeeping, and pig keeping. And naturally, a goddess who can give such valuable gifts can take them away again if she is angry. She might, in fact, do the same sorts of things of which historical witches were accused—cause blights, plagues, and crop failures.

Also rather like witches were some of the ancient storm goddesses and their descendants in folklore. One of these is Holde, a north German goddess originally associated with sky and winter. Feathers from her bed were said to be the snow, and she rode through the sky on the wind. After the arrival of Christianity, however, Holde became a witch and her name was used to frighten children. A similar figure in the folklore of southern Germany is Berchta. Once a gentle goddess who wore a mantle of snow and protected the spinners of wool, she later became a terrible ogress who ate naughty or lazy children. Berchta has very large feet and an iron nose.

Even more remarkable is Holde and Berchta's Russian cousin, Baba Yaga. She lives in a house that stands on a great pair of rooster legs and turns round and round. Her house is protected by a fence with a skull on the top of each picket. When she travels, she rides in a mortar steered by a pestle and sweeps away the marks of her flight with a broom. (Remember how Shakespeare's weird sisters sailed the seas in sieves.) In some stories, Baba Yaga's legs are too long to fit into her house, so that they are bent to fit the corners inside, and her ears drag on the ground. She cooks and eats people, preferring children. She, too, began life as a storm goddess, which may help us to see why historical witches were accused of raising storms and controlling the weather.

The connection of witches with pagan goddesses is underlined by their habit of eating children. The idea of the cannibal ogress is extremely ancient, and psychiatrists (doctors who treat mental disease) have suggested that it comes from a universal experience of very young children. Nursing babies suck milk from their mothers, but must learn not to bite. Biting hurts Mama. What if she got angry and bit back? Babies know they are small and helpless. When they grow bigger, they still vaguely remember the fear of the big, angry mama who might eat them up. Then the stories they tell each other become filled with witches who eat children and perhaps, like Hansel and Gretel's witch, tempt children with delicious but forbidden goodies such as candy houses.

Other beings who may well have left their mark on fairy-tale witches (and also on the historical witch beliefs

A Valkyrie, as artist Arthur Rackham thought she might appear. The winged helmet indicates her ability to fly through the sky, the spear and armor show her warlike character.

described in the next chapter) are the Norse Valkyries— armed maidens who carried those who died bravely in battle to the afterworld of Valhalla. Since the Valkyries were supposed to choose those who would fall in battle, they were associated both with death and with prophecy. Many believed they had heard the Valkyries in their wild rides across the sky, and as early as the year 1022–23, Wulfstan, Archbishop of the English city of York, complained of Danish invaders and Anglo-Saxon traitors as "witches and Valkyries," thus giving us a fine example of the way pagan ideas were becoming attached to much older ideas about witches.

The fact is that folklore is not like, say, arithmetic, because it does not proceed logically. Old ideas get mixed up with new ideas; some things are forgotten while others are remembered; but there is a strong tendency for old ideas to keep cropping up in different forms, because people's feelings about such matters as life and death, fertility and blight, health and illness are so strong. Even today, we are paying tribute to customs that go back before Christianity every time we knock on wood, wish on the first star, or say "Bless you!" when someone sneezes.

It would not really be surprising, therefore, if some people in Europe had refused to give up "the Old Religion," even after many generations. That, at least, was the explanation of historical witchcraft that was favored during the witch-trial period.

There is another aspect of witchcraft and paganism

that needs to be considered here. Certain modern writers have pointed out that witchcraft may have been important for women at a time when most were denied education, forbidden to hold office or own property, and unable even to choose their own husbands. According to this point of view, what witchcraft offered was *power*, real or pretended. If everyone in your village *believed* you could bewitch them, you would feel important, you would be respected or even feared, instead of being nobody but Old Granny Robertson or the Widow Brown. The fear of witchcraft would ensure that at least some of your spells worked—people who had annoyed you really would suffer fainting fits or mysterious pains. In fact, you would feel a little like mild-mannered Clark Kent, knowing that at any moment you might step into that thatched cottage or phone booth and emerge as—SUPERWITCH!

There was also the fact that the fertility magic that certainly survived in rural areas (whether or not it was organized into a "witch cult," as the witch-hunters of Shakespeare's time feared) had always given a much greater role to women than Christianity did. In pagan mythologies, it is the Earth Mother, whether she is called Demeter, Cybele, Freya, Inanna, Ishtar, or Isis, who controls the dark matters of life and death, seed time and harvest, fertility and blight. In some cases, perhaps,

Fragment of a relief showing the Mesopotamian goddess Inanna (about 2400 B.C.). She grasps a cluster of dates, and flower stalks sprout from her shoulders, showing her connection with nature and fertility. Like Demeter and Isis, Inanna made a famous visit to the underworld and possessed magical powers. Memories of these traits may have inspired the association of the great goddesses with witchcraft in later times.

women never gave up the old knowledge of herbs and stones and waters. Even in fairy tales, one occasionally meets a "wise woman" who reverses the witch's spell or heals a magical wound, and it is hard to tell how she differs from the witch except that she uses her powers for good instead of evil.

That is not to say, of course, that witchcraft was an early version of the women's rights movement. There is no convincing evidence to support such a view, and it is unfortunate that some overenthusiastic writers on women's history have carried the idea much too far. It may well be true, though that certain women sought power through the Old Religion when they could not get it in their everyday lives.

But the position of women in the Middle Ages certainly does have a bearing on the development of witches. The need to replace the old fertility cults with a religion centered on God the Father brought to our culture a general hatred and fear of women (who had been so powerful in the pagan religions) that is only now, slowly, being reversed. Just as the old goddesses were made into fairy-tale witches, women themselves came to be regarded as weak and silly at best, sly and sinful at worst. In short, it is this lingering distrust of women that for many centuries made it impossible to imagine a witch (the primitive, ill-wishing kind) as anything but a woman.

6

The Hammer of Witches

We know now that witchcraft is very old and that witch beliefs have taken many forms. Thus we are in a better position to understand outbreaks of witchcraft accusations in our own Western society, where several hundred thousand persons were executed for witchcraft in the 1500s and 1600s. Laws making witchcraft a crime were in effect in England until 1736, in Ireland until 1821. The last known burning of a European witch took place in Poland in 1793, although the action was illegal because witch trials had been done away with there in 1787.

There is no set date for the beginning of the madness called the witch trials in Europe, for there had been occasional accusations of witchcraft for centuries. Nevertheless, many people find it convenient to say that the witch mania began in 1486. That was the year of publication of an extraordinary book entitled, in Latin, *Malleus Maleficarum*, which means the Hammer of

The Latin title page of the Malleus Maleficarum *as published in London in 1669.*

Witches. That is exactly what the book's authors intended it to be—a hammer that would smash and destroy the supposedly terrible menace of witchcraft.

The book's authors were both Dominican monks and famed for their scholarship. One, Jakob Sprenger, was Dean of Cologne University in Germany; the other,

Heinrich Kramer, was prior (head) of an important religious community. The two men wrote the *Malleus* as a sort of "red alert" to judges, churchmen, and government officials, warning them that the threat of witchcraft was spreading and that witches must be ruthlessly hunted down and destroyed wherever they might be found.

The *Malleus Maleficarum* was divided into three parts. The first was a lengthy sermon on the vileness of the crime of witchcraft and a summons to join the crusade to destroy it. The second described the various types of witchcraft (called *maleficia*, or evildoing) and related the habits and customs of witches. The third part gave instructions for arresting, trying, and convicting witches. In all this, two things were especially noteworthy. The *Malleus* insisted that witchcraft was the use of *any kind* of spell, magic, or incantation, for whatever purpose, and was always inspired by the Devil. Furthermore, it asserted that to disbelieve in witchcraft was a heresy (religious crime) punishable by death. These opinions may not sound very remarkable, but in fact they were something rather new, and they brought death to many thousands of persons who would not otherwise have been executed.

As it happens, even the idea of the Devil was not a really ancient one. The early Hebrews who wrote the Old Testament (the Jewish Torah) barely mentioned

Satan and do not appear to have had any very clear idea of a great and powerful being who was opposed to the works of God. The Christian church did not adopt the notion of the Devil until A.D. 447, at the Council of Toledo, and even then the Devil was not linked closely to witchcraft.

In the 1200s, the official Church view of witchcraft was to be found in a document called the *Canon Episcopi* (or Bishop's Canon), which stated firmly that those who thought they had seen or been attacked by witches were victims of fantasies, dreams, or delusions. Far from making witchcraft a crime, the *Canon Episcopi* said it was heresy to *believe* in witchcraft. If this law had continued in force, it would have been impossible to convict most of the witches tried two centuries hence because the witnesses against them would have been declared heretics for merely believing witchcraft was possible.

Unfortunately, in 1484 the authors of the *Malleus* persuaded Pope Innocent the Eighth to reverse the *Canon Episcopi* by declaring that witchcraft was not only a great sin but a great heresy. Innocent's ruling was not the first Church document to take this view, but it had a much greater effect than earlier statements because it was a papal ruling (called a *bull*) rather than a mere opinion, and because it was later included in *Malleus Maleficarum*, which was a printed book. Printing was just coming into wide use at the time, and Innocent's bull was thus read by many more people than had ever had access to the few hand copies of previous documents. The *Malleus* quickly became something like a modern best-seller, going into at least twenty-nine editions before 1669, as well as being translated into German, French, Italian, and English.

And just what was it that made Sprenger and Kramer, the authors of the *Malleus*, so terribly upset about witchcraft that they would write a book urging all the churchmen and rulers of Europe to wage war against it? As it happens, we know quite well what Heinrich Kramer had been doing just before he sat down to write his part of the book, and it is not a story that makes us believe very strongly in the menace of witches or in the standards of justice recommended for witch trials.

As soon as Innocent's bull against witchcraft was issued, Kramer traveled to the Tyrol, a part of Austria, and demanded that its ruler and its bishop (Archduke Sigismund and the Bishop of Brixen) help him search out and prosecute witches. As a result, an accusation was made against the archduchess, who was said to have used witchcraft and poison against her husband. On several occasions, a mysterious voice spoke out against her and certain other court ladies, mostly friends of the archduchess. Some of the courtiers present at the time dismissed the mysterious voice and said that in their opinion it belonged to someone hiding in the great palace ovens. They named the suspected speaker, the wife of a certain man named Geckinger. The story sounds very much as if someone about the court were conducting a rather clumsy hoax.

That, however, was not how Heinrich Kramer saw things. He already believed in witches—that much is clear. And he seems to have reached the foolish but dangerous conclusion that since witches were real, anyone accused of witchcraft must indeed be guilty. Far from dropping the case, he had some of the accused ladies arrested and tortured.

The archduke allowed it, but the Bishop of Brixen objected that the evidence was probably a fraud. The bishop ordered Kramer to leave the area. Kramer ignored him. Only when the bishop wrote that the menfolk of the accused ladies were looking for Kramer with vengeance in mind did the prior give up his campaign against the supposed witches in the archducal court.

Evidently, however, he never forgave the Bishop of Brixen, for the *Malleus Maleficarum* is full of nasty remarks about halfhearted churchmen who are not harsh enough in prosecuting witch cases. In the end, Kramer may have had his revenge on the bishop, as more than a few churchmen and officials were executed during the next few centuries for the doubtful crime of failing to arrest and burn enough witches in their districts.

We cannot know exactly how much the popularity of the *Malleus* contributed to the widespread witch persecutions that followed. (Certainly it was not the only cause, as is shown by the enthusiasm with which the book was received.) Nevertheless, it is fair to say that after 1486 it was open season on witches, on those suspected of witchcraft, and on certain harmless but unpopular minorities who could now safely be accused as witches.

At first, witch trials came singly or in small batches, but all too soon judges began to find that the accused numbered in the dozens or hundreds. Even at the time, some people were horrified at the sheer number of those put to death. A writer in Wolfenbüttel, Germany, observed in 1590, "The place of execution looked like a small forest from the number of stakes"; and in 1631, Cardinal Albizzi wrote of his trip to Cologne, Germany, "A horrible spectacle met our eyes. Outside the walls of many towns and villages, we saw numerous stakes to which poor, wretched women were bound and burned as witches."

The records of those centuries of witch trials run to thousands of pages, perhaps even hundreds of thousands of pages, and make horrifying reading. Here is one example from the records.

In the first half of the 1600s, the German city of

Bamberg was seized with a witch mania that lasted for decades. Prince-Bishop Johann Gottfried von Aschhausen burned about three hundred persons for witchcraft between 1609 and 1622 (one hundred two persons in 1617 alone). His successor, Prince-Bishop Johann Georg the Second, worked even harder and gained the title of Hexenbischof, which means Witch Bishop. In 1627, he had a special witch prison built in the city, large enough to hold thirty or forty accused witches at a time.

The witch persecutions began in Bamberg when one or two individuals who cured or cursed their neighbors were arrested on suspicion of witchcraft, tortured into naming others, and burned. Meanwhile, an ever-widening circle of those accused were in their turn arrested, tortured into accusing others, and so on.

Laws on torture in witchcraft cases varied widely at this time. In England, torture was forbidden; in most other places it was permitted if the judges so ordered; in Germany, it was required. No witch could be executed without a confession; and so, since the prisoners' guilt was usually taken for granted, it became *necessary* to torture them before sentence could be carried out. Many people quite sincerely believed that it was better for the souls of the accused that they should be tortured into confessing in this world, rather than suffering eternally in hell. In some cases, judges actually wept as they pleaded with the accused to confess.

So the arrests and tortures went on in Bamberg, but somewhere something got out of control. Most witch cases tended to burn themselves out after a certain number of executions, probably because people in general began to feel safer after the deaths of the "witches" who had supposedly been menacing their health and safety. (Much the same thing happened in some, by no means all, primitive witchcraft cases after a visit from a witchfinding group such as the Bamucapi.) But in Bamberg the fires, instead of burning out, only flared up more strongly. Accusations reached the highest levels of society, and neither the most prominent officials nor their families were safe from arrest, trial, and execution.

One of the very few persons who tried to stop the trials was Bamberg's vice-chancellor, Dr. Georg Haan. His efforts brought him to the attention of Witch Bishop Johann Georg the Second, and instead of being listened to, Dr. Haan was arrested, along with his wife and daughter, and burned as a witch in 1628. Anyone who could advise mercy or even moderation in dealing with witchcraft must be a friend of witches or even a witch himself, so ran the crazed logic of the executioners. *All* the burgomasters (chief magistrates or judges) of the city were eventually accused and condemned also, as were many other leading citizens.

One of the burgomasters, Johannes Junius, wrote a heartrending letter to his daughter from prison, and

Witches brewing up a hail storm, as shown on the title page of a book published in 1489 by Ulrich Molitor, an early follower of Sprenger and Kramer and titled (in translation) Concerning Female Sorcerers and Soothsayers. *The book is in the form of a debate on witchcraft, and in it the* losing *side argues that if witches could control the weather, kings would disband their armies and hire witches to blast their enemies' crops. This sensible idea was overridden, however, and soon the witch hysteria was in full swing.*

that letter has survived to tell us something of what it was like to be an accused witch in the 1600s.

Many hundred thousand good-nights, dearly beloved daughter Veronica. Innocent I have come to prison, innocent I have been tortured, innocent I must die. For whoever comes into the witch prison must become a witch [that is, confess] or be tortured until he invents something out of his head. . . .

Here Junius describes how he had had his thumbs crushed and been hoisted up to the ceiling by a rope tied around his hands. The executioner then warned Junius privately that he had better think of something or other to confess and satisfy the judges because he would die if he was tortured further. Junius asked for time to consider, and thought up a fairly harmless story about meeting a girl in a meadow who turned herself into a goat (the Devil) and attacked his throat, insisting, "You shall be mine." He consented to become a witch and attended some sabbats (so ran Junius's confession), but recognized no one. The court was not satisfied. The judges wanted the names of his fellow witches. They threatened further torture. Junius agreed that he had seen the city's chancellor. It was not enough. He must give them more names or be tortured again. Exhausted, he named thirty or so others. They asked what other crimes he had committed. He said none. They threatened him again. Then he confessed to another batch of nonsense. He had been given some poison to use on his son but had poisoned his horse instead. He had made love to a demon woman. He had stolen some communion bread from a church to use at the sabbat. At last it was over. The letter to his daughter continues:

Now, dear child, you have all my confession, for which I must die. And they are sheer lies and made-up things. . . . For they will never leave off with the torture till one confesses something; be he never so good, he must be a witch. . . . Dear child, keep this letter secret so that people do not find it, else I shall be tortured most piteously, and the jailors will be beheaded. So strictly is it forbidden [to write letters] . . . Dear Child, pay this man [the messenger] a dollar. . . . I have taken several days to write this; my hands are both lame. I am in a sad plight. Good night, for your father Johannes Junius will never see you more. July 24, 1628.

In the margin of the letter is a postscript revealing that among those who had accused Junius under torture was that same Vice-Chancellor Haan whose crime was trying to stop the witch trials.

And still the terror continued in Bamberg. By 1631, a total of nine hundred persons had been executed, and some of the accusers had grown rich on property seized from the victims. It was only by the personal interference of the Emperor Ferdinand the Second that the outbreak was stopped. This does not mean, of course, that Ferdinand did not believe in witches. He only ruled that mere rumor or public opinion was not enough to convict a person of witchcraft and that the accused should not be refused the advice of lawyers, as had been the practice at Bamberg. It did not occur to Ferdinand to object to the use of confessions extracted by torture.

Yet witch trials went on whether torture was used or not. In England, where torture was forbidden and witches were hanged rather than burned (a comparatively merciful death), the people feared witches just as much as their European neighbors did.

One study of witchcraft accusations in the English county of Essex during the 1500s and 1600s had some interesting results. It showed that there was a pattern of events and a standard cast of characters in a typical witchcraft incident. Very often, an old or widowed woman would come to a neighbor's door to beg some food or ask the loan of a kitchen utensil and the housewife or farmer would send her away empty-handed. Soon after, someone in the family would fall ill or suffer misfortune, and then everyone would remember the old woman's curses or angry looks and, behold, another witch had been discovered. At the village of Castle Cary, around 1530, an old woman named Christian Shirston asked Isabel Turner for a quart of ale. Isabel refused the gift, and immediately, "a stand of ale of twelve gallons began to boil as fast as a crock on the fire." In a similar way, Joan Vicars refused Mother Shirston some milk and thereafter her cow became diseased and gave nothing but blood and water. Finally, Henry Russe also denied her a gift of milk, and found himself unable to make cheese until Michaelmas. (These may seem like small misfortunes when we remember what Shakespeare's weird sisters did to the husband of the woman who was ungenerous with chestnuts.)

As it happens, English laws about the treatment of the poor were changing at the time. Earlier, villagers had believed it was their duty to give charity to less fortunate neighbors, and anyone who refused to do so would have met disapproval and might have been the subject of a sermon in church the next Sunday. Even the old folktales had the same message. The ugly sisters or proud brothers of the heroine or hero are always the ones who refuse help to the mysterious old woman, only to have her give her magical gifts or advice to the helpful one.

But in the period of which we are speaking this old network of mutual help began to break down. There were new taxes to establish almshouses for the poor, and perhaps people felt they should not have to give charity when they had already been taxed. But it is clear that the old ideas had not died, either. The result was that many people must have felt guilty about the way they treated women like Mother Shirston, and the witchcraft accusations were one way for them to handle that guilt: for of course no one will blame you for refusing favors to a witch.

We can see the same thing happen in our own society today whenever we hear the opinion that the poor who receive money from public funds are "welfare chiselers," people who are cheating the government, rather than unfortunate individuals to whom we (the society) owe some assistance.

One of the most remarkable later developments in the history of English witchcraft was the rise of a man named Matthew Hopkins, who gave himself the title "Witch-Finder General." Hopkins, a not-very-successful country lawyer, found the way to fame and fortune when, in 1645, he roused his home village of Manningtree with the accusation that witches held a sabbat near his house every sixth Friday. He accused a one-legged old woman named Elizabeth Clarke, bullied her into identifying five other "witches," and soon had brought about the first in what was to be a long series

A picture from the 1600s of Matthew Hopkins and two of the "witches" he forced to confess, with their familiars.

of witch trials. At one point he made the sensational claim that he possessed a list of all the witches in England.

Hopkins developed certain methods that helped him to become successful in his new career. The legal definition of torture was quite vague in the 1600s, and Hopkins discovered what modern "brain washers" also discovered. It isn't really necessary to burn, cut, or mangle people in order to force them to confess whatever their captors wish. Hopkins did not torture his prisoners, as English law then defined torture. He simply kept them tied up in uncomfortable positions, woke them every time they fell asleep, or made them walk continually for periods up to three days. Not surprisingly, his victims confessed almost as quickly as those subjected to torture elsewhere.

Another of Hopkins's "achievements" was to simplify the process of discovering who was a witch. He didn't require much evidence, not even witnesses who claimed they had been harmed by witchcraft. Instead, he placed most of his faith in finding witch marks by pricking the accused with pins. A "witch mark," we should note, was supposed to be a mark made by the Devil at the time the witch entered his service. It could look like any normal blemish—a wart, scar, or mole—but the way to tell whether it was a witch mark was to stick a pin into it. If the person did not feel pain from the prick, then he or she was a witch for certain. Needless to say, that was nonsense. There are many reasons why a particular part of the body may not be sensitive to a pinprick. An example is the kind of callus one gets on one's feet. Furthermore, a person terrified by the threat of torture might actually become "numb with fright" because of reactions of the blood vessels and nervous system. Scar tissue also is sometimes insensitive, and then there are all kinds of permanent and temporary nerve injuries that can result in loss of feeling. All in all, a determined inquisitor could probably succeed in finding a witch mark on almost anyone if he really wanted to. This is only one of several ways in which the witch trials were arranged so that the prisoner could not win.

Hopkins and his hundreds of pins became so famous that many superstitions concerning witches recommend using pins to keep them away. In Wales, for example, it used to be the custom to keep three pins, three needles, and three nails in a jar of salt as a charm against witch-craft. And as recently as the 1920s, a man in Lawrence, England, was brought to court accused of pricking his neighbor in the arm with a pin because he was convinced she had bewitched his pig.

Another idea supported by Hopkins and others at this period was that in addition to or instead of a witch mark, witches had an extra nipple on their bodies, from which a demon or familiar might suck blood. In the two years following 1645, Hopkins was responsible for hanging at least two hundred "witches," some of whom lost their lives merely for the crime of "entertaining evil spirits," which meant keeping familiars. Since a familiar could be almost any small wild or domestic animal, and since the nipple for suckling it could be almost any mark or blemish (it didn't even have to be numb, like a witch mark), it is not surprising that Hopkins could successfully convict nearly anyone he chose. In the case of Elizabeth Clarke, for instance, Hopkins claimed that the familiars she suckled were a white dog, a greyhound, a polecat, and an imp.

Still another of Hopkins's favorite methods for witch-finding was "swimming." As a technique, swimming went back to pre-Christian times, but though Hopkins did not invent it, he placed more faith in it and used it more often than other witch finders. The accused had their hands tied to their ankles and were then thrown into a pond or river. Those who sank were proven innocent; those who floated (held up, perhaps, by the air trapped in their clothes) were found guilty. Clearly, the accused could not win. The "innocent" stood a good chance of drowning, though in some cases a rope was tied around the waist for rescue purposes. The "guilty" survived only to be convicted and hanged.

By July of 1645, Hopkins was in the town of Chelms-

"Swimming" as a test for witchcraft. The cart with the broken wheel is an example of the misfortunes believed caused by witches. The black sow and the swimming dogs doubtless represent demons on whom the threatened witches call for help.

ford, where by his efforts thirty-three suspected witches had been arrested. He was now growing rich, since the property of convicted witches formed part of his fee. Of the Chelmsford witches, five were found guilty but pardoned, eight were held for further investigation— four (aged forty, sixty, sixty-five, and eighty) died in prison, four were still in jail awaiting trial three years later—and nineteen were convicted and hanged. Only one was found not guilty by the judges, who were completely convinced of the virtues of Hopkins's witch-finding methods. One of the judges had the remarkable name of Sir Harbottle Grimston.

Among the accused witches of Chelmsford was a woman whom Hopkins had forced to confess that she had a familiar imp called Nan. Some of the townspeople were so outraged at her treatment and so convinced of her good character that they rescued her by force from the jail. After her release, she stated that "she knew not what she had confessed and had nothing she called Nan but a pullet [chicken] that she sometimes called by that name." Her story was written down by Bishop Francis Hutchinson. "My opinion," he commented, "is that when witch finders had kept poor people without meat [food] or sleep till they knew not well what they said, then, to ease themselves of their tortures, they told them tales of their dogs and cats and kittens." Bishop Hutchinson was no doubt right, but it was another year after the Chelmsford witch cases before the public turned against Hopkins because of his methods, the sheer number of his accusations, and the wealth he had acquired. He was forced to retire in disgrace and died of tuberculosis within the year.

7

Bring On the Devil's Armies!

It was another hundred years after the death of Matthew Hopkins before the witch trials finally faded away. One of the last and smallest outbreaks of witch mania is also one of the best known, largely because it took place in the American Colonies, in Salem, Massachusetts. Vast amounts have been written about the Salem witch trials, yet only twenty persons were executed. Matthew Hopkins would have sneered, and Witch Bishop Johann Georg would probably have arrested the Puritan magistrates and ministers on the grounds that they had been too merciful and must therefore be witches themselves.

Fortunately, by the middle of the 1700s witchcraft trials had become occasional curiosities rather than a nearly universal mania. The trials were bloody and they were horrifying, but in the end reading about them is boring because all the screams become the same scream, all the accusations become the same accusation, and all

This picture of the arrest of a witch first appeared in Harper's Magazine *in 1883. Artist Howard Pyle captured in imaginative detail the fear, suspicion, and potential brutality that must have attended such scenes for centuries.*

the burnings become the same burning.

Much more interesting is the simple question, why? Why did the persection of witches flare up all across

Europe at just this period in history? And why was the kind of organized witchcraft supposedly practiced at sabbats so different from anything found in fairy tales, classical sources, or primitive societies?

As we have seen, by the end of the witch trial period, "everybody" knew in detail how witches lived and what they did, partly perhaps through reading the hundreds of books and pamphlets, together with thousands of pages of trial records, that had come into existence as a result of the trials.

Most witches (so the story ran) were introduced to witchcraft in one of three ways. Some were brought up as witches by their parents. Some were invited to a sabbat by a friend or relative. And some were persuaded to become witches by the Devil himself. In any case, they all ended by making a pact with the Devil, that is, an agreement to give up Christianity and worship Satan instead. This pact might be a document signed in blood, a list of names in a great book, or just a simple spoken agreement. Often it ran for a certain number of years and could be renewed. Quite often, the Devil promised money, magical power, and pleasure in return for the witch's services.

In addition to using magic for their own personal ends, witches got together to work magic as a group. A small local band of witches was called a coven, and usually numbered thirteen. The Devil was always consid-

The figure often called "The Sorcerer," painted during the Paleolithic period in the Trois Frères cave in France. Note the clearly human feet, hind legs, and beard, combined with the features of various animals.

ered the leader of the coven. Often, however, the Devil was represented by an officer who stood in for him at the meetings and was assisted by the Lady or Maiden, a woman who played the Devil's mistress.

A word here about the Devil. The image of a man with horns and/or the head of a horned animal was certainly much older in Europe than the Christian idea of a horned Devil. In fact, one of the earliest known pieces of European art is a 15,000-year-old painting from the cave called Trois Frères in France that shows a man either disguised as or half-transformed into a horned beast and surrounded by engravings of wild animals such as horses, bison, reindeer, wolves, bears, and mammoths.

The Celtic god Cernunnos as shown on the Gundestrup Cauldron.

From somewhat more recent times, we know that the pre-Christian Celtic and Germanic peoples worshipped a horned god in a number of forms. One was the Celtic god Cernunnos, who watched over the welfare of herds and flocks.

Figures very much like Cernunnos are found in many other parts of ancient Europe as well. Thus the fact that a horned god was still revered in some out-of-the-way places need not have meant that anyone was worshipping the Devil, as such. But of course any churchman who heard rumors of a horned god would tend to jump to conclusions.

Witches were widely believed to travel through the air to attend their meetings, although the idea that witches flew on broomsticks did not arise until quite late. Early drawings of witches show them flying on forked sticks similar to the distaffs used in spinning wool, on shovels, on hayforks, or on other farm or kitchen tools. Occasionally the witches use demon horses or winged monsters, or fly unaided. Compare Shakespeare's weird sisters and their habit of sailing the sea in a sieve. In order to be able to fly, witches often smeared themselves with a magical ointment, whose recipe was, of course, given them by the Devil.

The four great sabbats took place at the beginning of May, August, November, and February, and those (allowing for changes in our modern calendar) are the dates of the four most important pagan Celtic festivals: Beltaine, Lugnasad, Samain, and Imbolc. (Other pagan religions had similar festivals, though with different names.)

Two of the above dates, at least, are still familiar to us. Beltaine, or May first, is May Day, which is celebrated by dancing around a tree or pole trimmed with flowers and ribbons. The custom is not only pretty and enjoyable, but goes back to pagan ideas about welcoming back the goddess of summer and ensuring that fields and herds are fertile.

The celebration of Samain, November first, begins on October 31—and that, of course, is Halloween. The name means the eve of the Feast of All Hallows, a time when pious Christians honored the worthy dead, but when imps, sprites, spooks, and goblins were believed to be freed from the underworld to work mischief on the living. It is no wonder that Samain has survived in the modern world as the one night most closely associated with witches. It was considered to be the first day of winter, that is, the day on which the warm, life-giving sun annually lost its battle with the cold and dark of winter, and when storm witches like Berchta, Holde, Baba Yaga, and the Valkyries might be especially active. At such a time it was reasonable to think the universe might be in turmoil, and that normal boundaries—between the dead and the living, the past and the future, men and women, young and old, or one person's property and another's—might easily break down. That is why Halloween is the traditional time for ghosts to walk, for telling fortunes, for wearing disguises, for tricks, begging, and petty mischief, and for children to make demands on their elders. A similar but lesser event occurs every twenty-four hours at midnight, which is known as the witching hour.

The central feature of the sabbat was reported to be feasting and dancing, with or without an orgy. In a great many primitive religions such actions are a magical way of making sure that the days to come will be filled with wealth and plenty. The idea is to imitate on a small scale what one wishes to happen on a large scale. Just as the image stuck with pins is thought to hurt the person, so the spectacle of the community eating, drinking, dancing for joy, and making love is expected to produce prosperity and happiness in the coming year.

Where, then, did all those popular ideas about witchcraft come from? In order to answer that question, let us first recall the pathetic words of Johannes Junius to his daughter: ". . . they will never leave off with the torture until one confesses something." Remember, too, Junius's account of the nonsense he was at last forced to admit, merely in order to be allowed to die. The accounts of the trials of Johannes Junius and thousands of other accused persons all point to the conclusion that the judges knew exactly what they expected to hear confessed, and went on torturing their victims until the confessions matched their expectations. This conclusion is borne out by the strange fact that if one reads a great many of the witch-trial records, one soon realizes that not only the answers, but *the questions* are remarkably alike. In many cases, it is clear that the questions had been written out ahead of time and the prisoner had only to answer yes or no. As any modern lawyer, police officer, or journalist will tell you, that is a very poor way to learn the truth from anyone. It is such a bad way, in fact, that the use of this type of "leading question," as it is called, is forbidden in our court system. That is because witnesses can easily be influenced to say, not what they actually saw or heard, but what the lawyer suggests they *might have* seen or heard. Thus a lawyer may ask a witness, "Did you see anyone at the scene of the crime?" but not, "Did you see a blond man in a black leather jacket at the scene of the crime?" Leading questions are known to be confusing even to sensible witnesses who want to tell the truth. Their influence on terrified witnesses under torture, who had already learned that no one was going to believe in their innocence, would naturally be far greater.

To some extent it seems that the people who ran the witch trials, especially the high churchmen like Jakob Sprenger, Heinrich Kramer, and Witch Bishop Johann Georg the Second, actually created the witchcraft mania themselves by leading their victims into confessing what they wished, or feared, to hear.

The most important reason why the trial judges feared witchcraft was that the Bible assured them that witches were as real as shepherds, physicians, and carpenters. The command of the Book of Exodus that "Thou shalt not suffer a witch to live" was one they took literally. And because, on the whole, the judges were educated men, they had also heard about witches from Latin or

Greek literature, such as the story of Thelyphron and the witches in Chapter Three.

Remember all the stray bits of genuine paganism that were certainly floating about in the more out-of-the-way parts of Europe, as we saw in Chapter Five and in the discussion of the Devil, above. There was also the ancient, primitive fear of witches as unidentified enemies of society. Together, they provided the kindling that would set afire the witch mania.

Still, a fire needs both kindling and a spark. In the case of the witch trials, the spark that set them off was most probably the arrival of the Reformation. The term refers to the time when many individuals and some nations broke away from the Roman Catholic Church because they believed its practices, though not its basic Christian beliefs, needed to be reformed. Whereas in 1500 there had been in Western Europe "one holy, catholic, and apostolic church," by the end of the century there were many churches, Protestant (that is, Reformist) and Catholic. Lutherans, Calvinists, Puritans, Anabaptists, Anglicans, and others disagreed not only with the Catholics, but with each other, and their disputes took place on the battlefield as well as in churches, parliaments, and throne rooms. In 1572, for example, French Catholics killed over 3,000 French Protestants in the St. Bartholomew's Day Massacre, and in other times and places Protestants fought and killed Catholics just as brutally.

Nothing could have been more tragic and pointless than the death and destruction that were carried on in the name of religion at this period, but these events do serve to show us how very passionately people cared about religious matters during those times. It was only a short step from going to war with people because of their religion to believing that one's opponents, either Catholic or Protestant, were not in fact fellow Christians, but agents of the Devil. That people sometimes *did* feel that way is shown, for example, by the language of the First Scottish Covenant, a religious and political document of 1557, which referred to the Scottish Calvinists as "The Congregation of Jesus Christ" and to their Catholic opponents as "The Congregation of Satan."

That phrase, "The Congregation of Satan," brings us right back to the subject of witchcraft. Because of this tremendous religious (and as a result, political) upheaval going on all around them, even ordinary people felt the world as they had known it was crumbling and that only the Powers of Darkness could be responsible. The fear and anxiety were felt by both sides equally, as indicated by the fact that witchcraft persecutions were conducted with great fervor in Protestant and Catholic countries alike.

When rulers and churchmen became caught up in the fear and anxiety of their times, they quite naturally sought an explanation in what they knew or believed about the world around them. Being pious, they had been taught that all evil comes from the Devil, and they concluded that the Devil's efforts to destroy mankind must be organized very much like the Church's efforts to save it. (*Which* church made little difference.) This is an important point. If the godly went to church, the witches must gather at sabbats. If priests prayed at the altar, evil persons must perform human sacrifice on theirs. If God was assisted by armies of angels in heaven and a corps of churchmen on earth, the Devil also must have the services of armies of demons and a corps of witches. In short, the judges feared the worst; and to some extent, they not only tortured many innocent persons into confirming their fears, they made a reality of their own nightmares. For the evidence is strong that before the witch-trial period there was no widespread, organized cult of Satan or any plot to restore paganism in Europe at all.

(In this connection it is interesting to note that the word "sabbat," in the sense of a witches' equivalent of the Christian Sabbath, is not found in the English language until 1652, and "coven" not until 1662, indicating that the very idea of witch gatherings was a rather late development. The situation is similar in other European languages.)

There clearly was no plot *in the beginning*, then. But we must remember that the witchcraft trials lasted for over two hundred years and became the talk of all Europe. Now, policemen everywhere know that sensational crimes are often imitated. We can see this peculiar aspect of human nature at work when, no sooner is one airplane hijacked, one politician held hostage, or one person poisoned by a bottle of drugstore pain reliever, than the authorities have to cope with a whole rash of similar crimes. There is no reason to think things were different during the witch-trial period. As soon as tales of sabbats and Devil worship became well known, there were bound to be some individuals who tried witchcraft for thrills.

Consider what happened at the royal court of France between 1679 and 1682. It began with a police investigation of several poisonings among the rich and noble families of Paris. A fortune-teller named Marie Bosse boasted before witnesses that she had other sources of income besides predicting the future and that her clients were "nothing lower than duchesses, marquises, princes, and lords," adding, "Three more poisonings, and I retire, my fortune made!" In an operation rather like an undercover detective action on TV, a woman police agent bought some poison from Marie Bosse, claiming she wanted to get rid of her husband. Bosse and four others were arrested and questioned. Soon a web of accusations and counteraccusations involved not only many prominent nobles but King Louis the Fourteenth's own mistress, Madame de Montespan.

Witnesses confessed that de Montespan and several others had secretly celebrated Black Masses that were indeed vile imitations of religious services and involved the murder of babies. The object of the ceremonies was in most cases to gain benefits from the Devil—wealth, success in love, or the King's favor. The confessions, to be sure, were obtained by torture and thus legally suspect; but in this case there was more. The police searched the homes of the accused fortune-tellers and discovered a lavish supply of poisons, books on magic, wax figures, black candles, and other incriminating evidence. As a result, three hundred nineteen persons were arrested, of whom thirty-six were sentenced to death, thirty-four were banished, and four were condemned to slavery in the royal ships. We may say, then, that historical witchcraft, though it began in myth, fear, and religious upheaval, ended, in some cases, as a horrible truth.

Like thousands of other accused witches, the suspects in the Marie Bosse case confessed. Should we then conclude that there were other cases (even a tiny minority) where people were actually attempting to practice a Satanist version of witchcraft with evil intentions? Human nature being what it is, there probably were such cases, although we will never know exactly which ones they were.

There is more than one reason why some of those who confessed may actually have believed they were witches, however. For the first, we need only look at the "witch ointments," some of whose ingredients are given in the trial records. They include such substances as aconite, belladonna, and hemlock (the same hemlock found in the cauldron of Shakespeare's weird sisters). All come from plants commonly found in Europe, and all are poisons. If absorbed from the ointment by the body, they could produce some very real symptoms such as irregular heartbeat, numbness, partial paralysis (inability to move), and hallucinations ("seeing things"). Thus some, at least, of those who confessed to having flown to the sabbat may really have believed they had done so. Having heard about witch ointments from the publicity surrounding the trials, some foolish persons, like drug users today, may have tried the stuff "for kicks." Their confessions may be among the relatively small number obtained without torture, although it is hard to know how many of those were made by another type of person, who is familiar to modern police—the

94

one who will confess to the most horrible crimes in order to get attention. Some of the eager confessors to witch-craft were clearly just publicity seekers, while some, un-doubtedly, were mentally ill.

Similarly, if some of the accused truly believed them-selves to be witches, it is probable that some of the ac-cusers were honestly convinced they were victims of witch attacks. We've already seen that in primitive so-cieties fear of witchcraft can actually kill, and modern doctors who specialize in mental health are familiar with the fact that fear, in the form called hysteria, can pro-duce very real and frightening symptoms in its victims. Among the more common effects of hysteria are pa-ralysis of the arms and/or legs, the feeling of not being able to breathe, rapid heartbeat, blindness, inability to speak, mysterious pains with no visible cause, and faint-ing. It is typical in such cases that the patients imme-diately get better if they can be convinced that the threat has been removed. It is not surprising, therefore, that in a fear-ridden period like that of the witch trials some of the accusers should have suffered real illness as a result of their terror of witchcraft.

A fine example of this sort of situation occurred at the witch trials of Salem, Massachusetts, wherein a group of hysterical young girls became literally ill in the pres-ence of the "witches," but were "cured" as soon as the

A scene from the Salem witch trials painted by Howard Pyle. The acccuser at the right sees "a flock of yellow birds" around the head of the accused (standing, center).

accused were imprisoned. (Not all the Salem girls were hysterical, however. Some later confessed to deliberate fraud.)

There are also various diseases that probably played a role in starting accusations of witchcraft and of "possession" by demons. One of the strangest is Tourette's syndrome, a condition of the nervous system in which the patients may do nothing but imitate the words and actions of those around them, or may constantly feel compelled to use foul and violent language. Other, more common conditions are epilepsy, in which the patient suffers convulsions; narcolepsy, in which the patient falls suddenly asleep; and cerebral palsy, in which speech and body movements are jerky and poorly coordinated. It was certainly difficult for people of those times to understand how such symptoms could be anything but the work of the Devil.

In recent years, some researchers have suggested that at least a few witchcraft outbreaks may have had a different sort of cause. There is a fungus called ergot that grows on various grains in wet weather. If people or animals eat grain or grain products with ergot in it, they can develop alarming and mysterious cramps, spasms, and hallucinations somewhat like those of LSD. In earlier times, the disease was called St. Anthony's Fire, and records show witches were sometimes blamed. Certainly it is possible that occasional outbreaks of witch mania were caused by ergotism (it has been proposed that the Salem case was one of them). But that is a long way from saying witchcraft in general, with its thousands of years of history, can be explained in that way.

No, witchcraft was much more than paganism, hysteria, disease, ergotism, or even greed and envy. In fact, we can now see that by declaring "There's going to be a terrible outbreak of witchcraft," Sprenger, Kramer, and their colleagues were making a classic self-fulfilling prophecy.

8

Satanists, Keep Out

Even though it is a relatively short time since witchcraft was a crime, there are modern-day men and women who call themselves witches. Not that today's witches could exactly be called publicity seekers. After the events of the last few hundred years, no one can blame them if they keep their meetings *very* private, sometimes conceal their beliefs even from their friends and families, and hardly ever put ads in their local newspapers saying the equivalent of, "The July sabbat of the Middletown coven will be held at midnight on the night of the full moon in Barker's Meadow. All welcome."

Nevertheless, the recent growth of interest in mysticism and the occult has led a few, a very few, witches to allow themselves to be interviewed and to publish some information about their beliefs and practices. It is not easy, as it turns out, to separate the true witches from the thrill seekers, phonies, and mere dabblers who call themselves witches. However, a large number of self-styled witches agree to this: they are not Satanists, and they do not even believe in the Devil as such, although Satanism is potentially harmful. Above all, Satanists have no right to call themselves witches.

It seems history is on the witches' side in the argument, since we saw in Chapter Six that Satanism (the worship of the Devil) was largely invented by the accusers during the witch trial period and that the sort of nastiness of which Madame de Montespan and her colleagues were accused had little to do with the worship of the pagan goddesses who later became our fairy-tale witches.

Most modern witches, in fact, make a very clear distinction between the Craft, as witchcraft is often called, and the selfish and harmful magic of Satanists. In describing the difference, many witches say that Satanist magic is "of the left-hand path," while the magic of the Craft is "of the right hand." In this chapter, the word "witchcraft" should be clearly understood not to include Satanism.

One way in which the Craft differs from most more familiar religions is that it doesn't use any standard rituals, has no fixed beliefs, and varies widely in practices from one group and even from one individual to another. There is no single organization to which witches belong, although there is one fairly large group that calls itself Wicca after the Anglo-Saxon word meaning wisdom that is often said (although probably mistakenly) to be the root of our English word witch. Wiccans and other witches do appear to agree on a few basic facts about witchcraft as it is practiced today, however:

1) Witchcraft is a religion.

2) Witches worship a goddess who is most often referred to simply as "the Lady," although she has dozens of other names. With her is "the Horned God," and both are deities of nature and fertility.

3) Witches meet together for the four great sabbats, described in Chapter Seven. Lesser meetings, held weekly or monthly, are called esbats.

4) A group of witches that meets regularly is called a coven, and the ideal makeup of a coven is thirteen members: six couples and an additional member of either sex.

5) The coven member who is generally acknowledged as the wisest and most experienced is the coven's priest or priestess and plays the role of the god or goddess during ceremonies.

6) Witches do not use the term "warlock" for a male witch and are apt to giggle inwardly whenever they hear the term. Male or female, a witch is a witch.

7) In order to become a member of a coven, a can-

didate must be initiated. Initiation is only granted after months, more often years, of serious study and is definitely not open to those in search of fun or thrills. Witches believe that magic is a tool to be used responsibly and wisely. They would no more trust their secrets to a novice than they would let a five-year-old drive a car.

8) A coven meeting very often takes place inside a nine-foot circle inscribed on the ground or floor. Symbols of the four directions and of the four elements (earth, air, fire, and water) are often found on the altar within the circle or at the cardinal points outside it.

9) Inside this magic circle, the coven raises what witches refer to as "the cone of power," a sort of combined psychic field by which the group works its magic.

10) Some of the purposes for which the coven uses its power are healing, blessing, and protection (the last in case of attack by Satanists or other evil forces). Magic is done for members, for other witches or covens, and occasionally for nonwitches who seek the coven's help. The coven must be satisfied that any outsider's request is both urgent and proper. If you want your boyfriend to stop seeing that other girl or your boss to break a leg, forget it.

11) Neither covens nor individual witches use their powers for their own material advantage (predicting the

winners of horse races, or the rise and fall of the stock market, for instance). They say there is something about magic that destroys it when used selfishly.

12) Covens spend a good deal of their time working spells for the purification and fertility of the earth in general. Their aims have much in common with those of the environmental movement, and one group of witches even reportedly has a ritual for general use on Earth Days.

These few points seem to cover the essentials of witch beliefs. There are also some attitudes that are very commonly found among witches, although they are probably not universal. One is the belief in reincarnation, the idea that the soul is immortal and is reborn in a series of bodies. Another is the acceptance of various occult and fortune-telling techniques such as astrology, card reading, palmistry, numerology, and whatever else seems to suit the individual witch's fancy.

Though witches insist in all seriousness that magic must be used responsibly, they are not above giving tit for tat when they believe they are being pushed around. Journalist Susan Roberts was interviewing a self-proclaimed witch named Joe Lukach when he learned that the superintendent of his apartment building was demanding a bottle of vodka for the return of a valuable ring Mr. Lukach had lost on the premises. Without a word of protest, Lukach sent out for a bottle of vodka, performed a few magical operations on it, and handed it over to the super. You and I will have to decide for ourselves whether it was sheer coincidence that from that day on, according to Ms. Roberts, the superintendent lost favor with his bosses, made a series of costly errors, and was later fired for drinking on the job. Even if witchcraft was not involved, the fact that the vodka, or something much like it, led to the man's downfall was certainly a case of the punishment's fitting the crime.

Joe Lukach identifies himself as a *traditional witch*, but traditional witchcraft is by no means the only branch of the Craft practiced today. There are in fact four "schools" of modern witchcraft—hereditary, traditional, ceremonial, and Gardnerian.

Hereditary witchcraft is the easiest to explain, as a hereditary witch is simply one who learned the Craft from a relative who was a witch or who, perhaps, believes he or she inherited a knowledge of the Craft from a witch ancestor. Some hereditary witches insist that they are the only true witches, since a witch is born, not made. Others, however, go on to become initiated into covens of any of the other three types.

Probably the best-known hereditary witch of our day is an Englishwoman named Sybil Leek, who traces her ancestry back through a long line of British and Russian witches. Mrs. Leek has written many books on the subject of witchcraft. One of them, *Diary of a Witch*, is an amusing and readable autobiography in which she tells of her life as a witch and of learning witchcraft from her grandmother. It and Susan Roberts's *Witches, U.S.A.* are probably the best full-length books for the beginner who wants to know more about the lives of some real, modern witches.

Traditional witches may or may not be hereditary witches also, as we said above. Traditional witches practice the Craft according to the rules and customs handed down in various areas of the Western world. Some of the traditions best represented among American witches are the Celtic, the Germanic, the Italian, the Hungarian, the Spanish, the Scandinavian, and the Slavic, but there are many others. Voodoo could almost be called an African form of traditional witchcraft, but Voodooists worship a different set of gods from those of the witches—gods who accept animal sacrifices. Modern witches are opposed to animal sacrifices because of their ideas about reincarnation and their belief that the Craft exists to enhance, not to destroy, the life force.

Ceremonial witches, by contrast, are those who, while often believing in the witch religion, practice *magia*, which is an ancient, complex, and obscure form of magic largely based on a Jewish system of biblical interpretation known as the Cabala (or Kabbalah). Witches are quick to point out, however, that ceremonial magic may be used by people who do not follow the witch religion and who should be called ceremonial magicians, rather than witches. Mastering ceremonial magic can take a lifetime of study, and it is rare to find more than one or two ceremonial witches in any one coven. Witches have a deep respect for ceremonial magic, but they believe that just because it is so powerful, it can be seriously misused, with harm to the user as well as to others. Ceremonial magic is not evil in itself, like Satanism, but it resembles a hefty charge of explosive—you may blast a railway tunnel through a mountain with it, or you may start a landslide that destroys a whole town.

Most witches would probably agree that the greatest ceremonial magician (not witch) of our time was Aleister Crowley. Born in England in 1875, Crowley grew up in a family of extremely strict Christians. Although he was probably no more mischievous than any other boy of his age, Crowley's mother came to believe he was the Antichrist, a sort of Devil in human form. The sad thing is that young Crowley came to believe it too. Crowley decided, at an early age, that if he was evil already, he might as well be *very* evil. In later years, he delighted in calling himself "The Wickedest Man in the World"

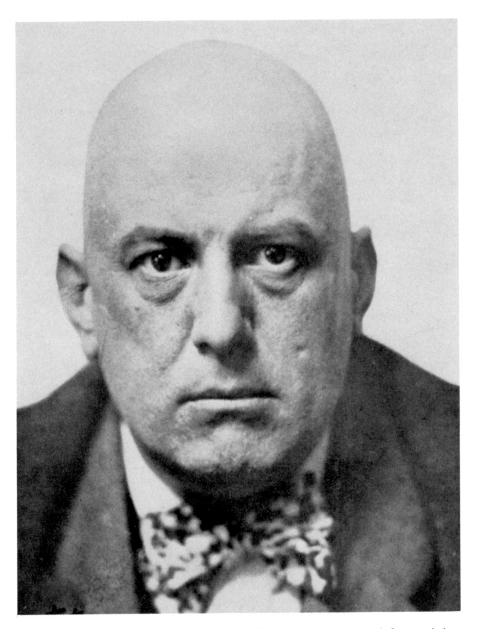

"The Wickedest Man in the World," British ceremonial magician
Aleister Crowley in his later years. How pleased Crowley must have
been that in this picture and some others his ears appear distinctly
pointed!

and in creating scandals to match the title. He studied yoga, the teachings of Oriental mystics, and especially the contents of various *grimoires*. A grimoire is a magical textbook much used in ceremonial magic, and many, if not all, grimoires are devoted to magic of the left-hand path. Instead of invoking the forces of peace, healing, fertility, and harmony, as witchcraft claims to do, grimoires give instructions for calling up demons and forcing them to do the magician's will. Grimoires have impressive and mysterious titles such as *The Grand Grimoire*, the *Grimorium Verum*, *The Key of Solomon the King*, and *The Book of the Sacred Magic of Abramelin the Mage*, and contain much information on the supposed power of numbers, words, gems, colors, metals, symbols, and diagrams. Crowley's studies eventually led him to found his own mystical organization, which he called the Order of the Silver Star, and whose motto was, "Do what thou wilt shall be the whole of the law." Although Crowley was a recognized poet, scholar, student of languages, and (oddly enough) mountain climber, he ended his days as a half-mad drug and alcohol addict, convinced that his person and his actions were divine. Sybil Leek, who knew Aleister Crowley when she was a child, believes that he might have become one of the great witches of all time, but that he sold out to the evil forces he invoked.

In 1953, only six years after the death of Aleister Crowley, another Englishman published a book, called *Witchcraft Today*, and became the founder of the fourth major division of modern witches, the Gardnerians. The witchcraft of Gardnerians differs from traditional witchcraft not so much in its beliefs as in its practices, and especially in its attitude to publicity. Its founder, Gerald Gardner, laid special emphasis on British archaeologist Margaret Murray's theory that witchcraft was the survival of European paganism. In 1921, Professor Murray published a book entitled *The Witch-Cult in Western Europe*. In it she argued that the organized, widespread kind of witchcraft confessed to at some of the witch trials actually was evidence of a secret, pagan religious cult that had gone "underground" in Europe after the arrival of Christianity.

We have already seen that there were plenty of pagan ideas and practices surviving in the form of remembered festivals, superstitions, folktales, memories of the Mother Goddess and the Horned God, fertility magic, and so on. Undoubtedly, churchmen were aware of this; undoubtedly, they disapproved, and very probably the existence of such beliefs fueled the witch mania when it came. Unfortunately, however, Professor Murray (and some of her followers) became much too enthusiastic in trying to prove the existence of "The Old Religion," as she called it. By the end of her career, she was arguing that these stray bits of paganism amounted almost to an international plot to overthrow the Church and that several important persons, such as Saint Joan of Arc and various kings of England, had been witches in secret. Researchers today are agreed that this is nonsense. Murray used evidence from ancient Egypt and the magical systems of the Near East, even though there was no good reason to connect the ideas of those places with early Europe.

Gardner and large numbers of modern witches (not all of them Gardnerians) agree with Murray that witchcraft was widespread and pagan in nature at the time of the witch trials. They are thus forced into the position that a considerable number of those convicted were guilty according to the law, though of course they also hold that the laws were wrong because witchcraft is harmless. Yet if that is so, they must be accepting as evidence those same confessions obtained under torture that seem so outrageous to us. My own opinion is that modern witchcraft is much more like a *revival* of paganism than a continuation of it. But the witches, naturally, do not agree.

Another important point of view of Gardner's was that he encouraged witches to speak out about their beliefs and to insist that witches had the same rights as followers of Buddhism, Islam, Hinduism, Judaism, Christianity, Taoism, or any other religion. Non-Gardnerian witches don't agree as to whether this was a good thing. Some feel that the extreme secrecy of the past was stifling. Others think that publicity in general only encourages thrill seekers and that the Gardnerians' brand of publicity in particular puts witchcraft in a bad light. Gardnerians sometimes pose for photographs in the nude, or "skyclad," as they call it. (The term is borrowed from Hinduism.) They assert that clothing hampers the flow of the body's energy field, but many other witches scoff at this notion and find the use of the term "skyclad" hilarious. Both groups are quick to declare that, nude or clothed, witch meetings are not orgies.

The fact that Gardnerians and non-Gardnerians (American ones, at least) don't get along too well is probably due to the Gardnerians' claim that *their* brand of witchcraft is the only true one. A few years ago, in fact, the English Gardnerians sent out "colonists" to bring witchcraft to the U.S.A., much to the annoyance of witches who were already here. Susan Roberts quotes one witch, who traces the Craft in his family back to the days of the American Revolution, as sighing, "Here come the British, out to rule the Colonials again."

The leading Gardnerians in America today are Dr. Raymond Buckland and his wife Rosemary, known as

Robat and Lady Rowen to the witch community. They were initiated into the Craft by Gerald Gardner himself, and before moving to Virginia, they ran the Buckland Museum of Witchcraft and Magick out of their Long Island home. It was patterned after a museum known as "The Witch's Mill," which was started by Gardner in Castletown on the Isle of Man, off the west coast of England. Though the various branches of the Craft may have their differences, it is clear that witchcraft is alive and well in modern society, and witches themselves are hopeful that the terror of the witch trials can never come again.

Certainly, witchcraft has become a great deal more "respectable" in recent years. As long ago as 1974, New York University offered the first of several very popular courses in witchcraft, and in 1975, the First World Congress of Sorcery was held amid considerable fanfare in Bogotá, Colombia, and attended by hundreds of witches, wizards, mages, sorcerers, conjurors, shamans, soothsayers, necromancers, thaumaturges, and exorcists, not to mention curious journalists and members of the public.

Before we congratulate ourselves on the progress the Western world has made since the 1600s, however, we might think back to some of the things we learned about primitive witchcraft in Chapter Two. Witchcraft as it is

Self-proclaimed modern witches perform a ring dance in the open air. It is only in recent decades that even a minority of witches have been willing to make their activities public.

practiced by Wiccans and others seems harmless enough in its emphasis on peace, health, and harmony in the natural world. But though modern witches rarely discuss the fact, we have seen the evidence that witchcraft can also be something very different—a practice that goes to the root of some of humanity's most basic fears.

To our earliest ancestors, witchcraft was the explanation of accident, misfortune, and tragedy, a natural response to the desire to blame *someone* for the unforeseen. And "witch" was the label given to the bad citizen, the enemy within the gates who smiled a false smile while secretly working harm to crops, beasts, and people. It would be a great mistake for us to think that just because we no longer worry about dolls with pins stuck in them, we are no longer prey to the fear of witches.

At least three times in this century, we have seen events suggesting that though the labels have changed, the ancient fear is still alive. Several scholars have pointed out the similarities between Hitler's campaign against the Jews in Germany before and during the Second World War and the treatment of accused witches during a typical witch hunt, whether in Africa, India, or Bamberg. First, all the tribe's or nation's troubles are blamed on the target group. In Hitler's Germany, the principal problems were inflation, depression, and unemployment. The worse the problems, the more tempting it is to find a scapegoat. And once the identity of the "witches" is known, it becomes every citizen's sacred duty to destroy them ruthlessly, without legal trials, without mercy, and without even a thought for the absurdity of the charges. Of course, anyone who protests the witch hunt will be accused in turn, like Dr. Georg Haan of Bamberg. Finally, even people who do not really accept the myth of witchcraft (or Jewish responsiblity for Gemany's troubles) will join the chorus of accusers in order to escape suspicion themselves. And so the terrible cycle goes on, and thousands or millions of innocent people are destroyed for crimes they never dreamed of committing.

The situation in the U.S.S.R. was almost exactly similar during the Communist purges under Stalin and later. An interesting addition to the scene was the insistence on obtaining public "confessions" from those accused of anti-Marxist thoughts or deeds. Poor Johannes Junius might almost have been describing Stalinist Russia when he wrote, "For they will never leave off with the torture until one confesses to something. . . ."

Not much less frightening was the anti-Communist campaign carried out by Senator Joseph McCarthy in this country in the 1950s. McCarthy even echoed Witch-Finder General Matthew Hopkins, with his supposed list of all the witches in England, when he claimed to possess a list of Communist Party members in the U.S. State Department. No one was burned at the stake or sent to a concentration camp by McCarthy, but citizens lost their jobs, their freedom, their livelihoods, and many of their Constitutional rights because one man was able to convince the nation that its economic and foreign-policy problems had been brought about by a secret and deadly group of enemies within.

Could the witch trials happen again? I doubt that witches or even Satanists would ever be the victims of a modern witch hunt, because a society that does not believe in magic cannot feel threatened by it. But as long as we are willing to blame our troubles on the sinister influence of other religions, races, nations, or political groups, we will be living with the possibility that the spirit of the *Malleus Maleficarum* is not dead.

The stories in this book are my own re-tellings of very old tales. "The Worst Witch Story of All" is contained in *The Golden Ass* by Lucius Apuleius. "The Old Witch" was first written down by the brothers Grimm in the early nineteenth century, although the story itself is surely much older.

The quotations from Johannes Junius that appear in Chapter Six may be found, among other places, in *The Encyclopedia of Witchcraft and Demonology* by Rossell Hope Robbins. The words of the Gusii tribesman quoted in Chapter Two were published in a collection of scholarly articles entitled *Witchcraft and Sorcery*, edited by Max Marwick. Those who would like to read more about the fatal effects of being bewitched talked about in Chapter Two can read G.W. Milton's 1973 study of such deaths.

Index

Page numbers in *italics* refer to illustrations.

117